Stark Realities

I0539324

Peter Carroll

Raven Crest Books

ISBN-13: 978-0-9931909-6-4

ISBN-10: 0-99-319096-0

For Sharon and Megan

1.

She can see the edge. It should frighten her but she doesn't feel scared. Maybe whatever she's taken is helping in that regard. It's hard for her to be sure. Standing there, waiting, she knows there is no way out. No alternative. It brings her a sense of peace, a sense of acceptance.

Sorry.

So very sorry.

When she goes over she can feel the air against her face, the twisting of her body as it falls through space. The sensation is odd, unnatural, like nothing she's felt before but not unpleasant. In different circumstances it may even have been thrilling.

She hits the water, goes under into black. The impact is dull, forceful. She's unprepared for such unyielding solidity and it knocks most of the breath from her. The cold clamps its icy arms around her but this is no reassuring hug, no lover's embrace. It doesn't feel like she's got the strength to fight it off. Even if she did, she's pretty sure she would still give in.

Hissing, roaring, gurgling noise rushes and swoops around her.

It has taken longer than she thought it might for this to come around. To get to this place, this moment. She deserves to be here. No-one would grieve if they knew but she never told anyone. How could she? The shame would be too great. A shame she's kept hidden, secreted about her conscience. A dark place no-one else visits. It's been her burden to carry. A self-inflicted wound that has festered and wept without any sign of healing.

Her limbs are heavy, failing to respond. She doesn't care anymore. It's time. It's way past time. The rest of the world will be better off without her.

The reflexive holding of what little breath survived the thumping contact with the surface is coming to an end. She's spinning and turning without any propulsion on her own part. The cold is starting to leave her, being replaced by a strange warmth.

Her eyes open to an endless, blurred murk and instantly close again.

The first breath inundates, causes coughing spluttering panic. She's changed her mind, she wants to fight. Perhaps this isn't the time after all. She's wracked with remorse, of course she is. Surely, that should be enough? Why wouldn't it be enough? Why would anyone demand more of her than genuine, heartfelt contrition? What is done cannot be undone. There's no denying her sorrow, her willingness to make amends. This shouldn't have to be her penance.

Sorry.

So very sorry.

She tries to muster arms and legs; invites them to join her in a race to the surface, but they don't seem to be interested, don't respond to her encouragement. She just keeps turning and choking, the warmth spreading through her like someone pulling a blanket up to her chin.

Two or three more breaths and the choking stops.

Her eyes open.

The murk and the cold no longer feel like adversaries. They are guides.

Despite the turbulence all around her, she feels calm; at one with all of this.

An apology would never be enough. This is what is required to make things right.

It *is* time.

Too late for changing minds.

This was inevitable. Only a matter of time.

Sorry.

So very sorry.

The hardest word, but such difficulty offers no consolation to the wronged.

This will be her penance after all.

She needs to go.

The dark closes in around her.

The water can carry her shame away, keep it hidden forever.

Sorry.

So

…...very

…................sorry.

2.

Stark's head thumped as if someone inside it was beating out the timpani at the start of *2001: A Space Odyssey*. The first attempt to prise his eyelids open ended badly. The second only marginally better. He tried to remember why this might be happening; tried to fathom which momentous occasion justified the onset of such an epic hangover. Nothing obvious sprang to mind. He sat up and put his elbows on his knees and cradled his pounding head in his hands – hankering for the days when his willpower and lifestyle maintained abstinence.

For many years Stark had sworn off the drink, only indulging when a toast or similar act of social etiquette required it. Since returning to Scotland from his long exile in London and, more specifically, since the death of his mother, sobriety in social situations had become rarer and rarer. More worrying was the prevalence of hangovers resulting from entirely unsocial drinking. He was pretty sure last night's session was a solo effort, conducted within the confines of his own home. He needed to get a grip.

The mobile phone danced on his bedside cabinet, the ringtone muted but the vibrate function engaged. Stark picked it up and looked at the caller ID.

"Ian. What's up?" asked Stark.

"We've got a body, sir. I'll be round to pick you up in ten minutes."

Detective Constable Ian Barr; such an enthusiast, such an optimist.

"Fuck me, Ian. I'm just up and nowhere near ready. Give me twenty. Okay?"

"Aye, no bother, boss. I'll see you then."

Stark ended the call and dropped the phone onto the

bed beside him. He flopped backwards, arms spread out. There were no nails in his hands but it felt like he might be wearing a crown of thorns. This really wouldn't do. Stark struggled up to his feet and trudged into the bathroom. The shower would help; as would a glass of water from the tap.

Once washed, dried and dressed, Stark went into the kitchen and gulped down another two glasses of water. There wouldn't be any time for tea or toast before the ever-prompt DC Barr arrived. He grabbed a couple of paracetamol and washed them down with more water. A wave of nausea and heat swept through him but it passed without incident.

A horn tooted as Barr swung the car around in front of his house. Stark grabbed a jacket and went out to join his colleague.

"Ooft, you look as rough as a badger's arse, sir! Heavy night was it?" asked Barr, the glee in his voice undisguised. He found it hilarious that his boss was such a lightweight drinker. As far as Stark could tell, Barr appeared impervious to the after effects of alcoholic over-indulgence.

"Aye, got to stop drinking on school nights. My head's bursting!"

"Were you out somewhere?"

"Naw, just in the house."

"Right," said Barr, surprise and maybe even a hint of disapproval in his tone. Barr had often expressed his surprise at Stark's former teetotal ways, finding it difficult to believe his boss could enjoy being so abstemious, but this newly-acquired, hard-drinking habit didn't suit Stark as far as Barr was concerned. The boss didn't appear to have the necessary constitution for it.

"Alright, Maw! Jeez, you'd think you never drink yourself. Anyway, what's the story with this body?"

"Details are patchy, sir. A young woman, washed up near Clackmannan. The DCI is already on his way down there."

"Great, that should help," muttered Stark, unable to prevent the jibe escaping his lips. Even if Barr did consider DCI Don McLaren as much of a dickhead as Stark did, it was never a good idea to bad-mouth a superior in front of the troops.

Barr smiled but said nothing.

Stark put on his seatbelt, then reached over and turned on the air conditioning. He wasn't feeling too clever at all.

The road took them through the small market town of Clackmannan and its quirky little square. From there the road wound downhill onto the flat floodplain of the River Forth – known locally as the Carse. As they descended along a road signposted to indicate it was designed with cyclists' welfare in mind, they could see the grey, snaking river widen to the east. For now, the giant power station at Longannet belched its usual plume of smoke. It's coat had been on a shaky nail for a while and now the owners had confirmed its imminent closure; a remnant of Scotland's pre-global-warming fossil fuel gluttony; soon to become a fossil itself. For the moment, rows of pylons marched out across the land like a giant's washing line awaiting clothes, carrying electricity to thousands of hungry appliances; and, on the southern side of the river, the flares at the oil refinery in Grangemouth scorched the chill morning air. They turned right off the single-track road and onto a narrow lane with a much rougher surface. After passing a small row of houses, with one or two uneasy-looking residents taking in the unfolding drama on their doorsteps, a ruined building came into view.

"What's that place, Ian? Some kind of castle?"

"No, sir. That's the Kennetpans Distillery, eh. It used to be really famous an' important but it's a wreck now, like. From what I heard, though, they're planning on doing it up an' turning it into a tourist attraction."

A few official vehicles were parked on an open, grassy area in front of the distillery. The SOCO team were there and Stark recognised McLaren's car parked next to a marked up squad car. The young PC who'd been allocated bouncer duties nodded as they decanted from the pool car Barr had used. The fresh air felt good. Stark's head finally began to give him some respite but his stomach still felt jittery.

"Alright, McKay? Where do we go?" asked Stark.

"You need to go round the back of the distillery there, sir, through that gap, eh" replied the young man, pointing to where he meant.

Stark still found that 'eh' thing that sounded more like 'ay' weird. What went wrong with adding 'ken' to the end of their sentences; like they did when he was growing up? At least it had character; allowed you to instantly place the user on a map, work out roughly where they might come from. 'Eh' seemed so generic, so bland.

"Right, ta."

Barr and Stark clambered over a section of broken-down wall and through the other side of the building. Reeds and scrubby trees gave way to a small, grassed area where the main action appeared to be going on. The SOCO team and DCI McLaren were gathered alongside a jetty – in a state of disrepair to match that of the tumbledown distillery. The river lapped gently at the shore as they picked their way through the reeds (and the rubbish deposited by the tide) to join the others.

The DCI looked around as they approached.

"Evening, Stark," he said, "glad you could join us."

It was only seven forty-five in the morning and, even if he hadn't had a monumental hangover, Stark could do without this kind of sarcastic pish.

"Aye, sorry, sir. We got stuck behind a couple of tractors," he lied. "What have we got?"

"Young lassie, probably aged twenty-something by the looks of her. No' sure how long she's been in the water, like, but that'll become apparent once the post-mortem's been done, eh."

"Jumper?" asked Barr.

"Too soon to tell, but maybe," replied McLaren

The Forth now had two bridge crossings nearby. The older Kincardine Bridge was built in the 1930's while the new Clackmannanshire Bridge was opened in 2008. This new bridge was closer and, from Stark's first impressions, seemed the more likely structure for someone to use when committing suicide.

Stark felt his stomach flip over and a cold sweat created a film across his lower back. A camera flash of memory lit up his mind – blind panic, stairs, a door, the pallid ghost that was once his twin sister. He struggled to contain his emotions but years of learning how to maintain professional detachment kicked in.

"Wouldn't surprise me, but let's not make any assumptions just yet," added Stark.

The girl was floating face down. Her long, blonde hair flowed out from the top of her head like a golden oil slick. She seemed to be fully-clothed, which indicated there was probably no sexual angle involved. She bobbed against the shore, snagged by a broken piece of the wooden jetty. Stark looked around, absorbing as much detail as he could, but nothing else seemed out of place.

"Who found her, sir?"

"A local guy. Birdwatching, apparently. He's over by the cars waiting to be interviewed, eh. I'll handle things here. You two go an' have a word wi' him."

"Okay, sir, will do."

"Where's the witness, McKay?" asked Stark.

"He's over there, sir," he said, pointing at a tall, spindly character standing about thirty metres away. "His name's Graham Gilbert. Local guy, says he was down here looking for birds."

"The two-legged variety?" quipped Barr.

"They've all got two legs, you muppet. Ever seen a bird wi' four legs?" replied Stark, rolling his eyes.

"Oh, aye, right enough. Doh!" said Barr.

"I assume he meant the feathered variety, sir," said McKay.

"Right, ta."

Graham Gilbert looked like a man who had just discovered his first ever dead body. His skin tone suggested a ravenous vampire had recently paid him a visit. He took rather short, feeble drags on his cigarette and exhaled the smoke without any obvious relish or gusto. Greasy, salt-and-pepper hair thinned out on top so as to barely conceal his scalp, while the beard was a poor excuse for facial hair. Scruffy, cheap clothes were at odds with the – presumably – very, expensive binoculars slung around his neck. As Barr and Stark approached he dropped the remains of the cigarette to the ground and crushed it under his toe.

"Mr Gilbert?" asked Stark.

The scruffy birder nodded.

"Hello, sir. I'm Detective Inspector Adam Stark and this is Detective Constable Ian Barr. If you don't mind, we'd like to ask you a few questions."

"Aye, that's fine. Bloody terrible, so it is. Just down here birding, eh. Canny believe it."

There was a tremor in his voice and he stroked his chin as he spoke.

"No, it's never nice stumbling across something like that," agreed Stark. "Now, I'll need some personal details from you an' then you can tell us what happened an' how you came to find the dead girl. Ok, sir?"

Gilbert shrugged and nodded.

Barr took out his notebook and pen and jotted down Gilbert's name, address, date of birth and telephone number. With that done, they commenced with the interview.

"Well, I was coming down here to do a bit of birding, you ken? You get some really braw sunrises at this time of the year and I knew the weather was going to be good, so I got here about five o'clock."

"How did you get here, Mr Gilbert?"

"By car. That's mine there," he said, pointing at a dark green Nissan Micra. The layer of grime and the battered wheel trims – one completely missing – were unsurprising features. Matching the standard of upkeep its owner demonstrated in relation to his own appearance.

"Did anyone see or hear you leave this morning?"

"No, I live on my own."

Barr smirked and Stark tried to ignore him.

"Ok, so you got here at five; then what did you do?"

Gilbert stroked his chin again and smoothed the strands of hair on top of his head before putting both hands into his trouser pockets.

"I had a wee cup of coffee – always bring a flask when I'm out and about. After that, I walked out behind the distillery and began to set up my scope to scan the river."

"Scope?" queried Stark. This was a world he was entirely unfamiliar with.

"Aye, telescope, so I can see things that are further away than my binoculars can manage; it's back in the car now, eh."

"Oh, right. Go on."

"Anyway, she just caught the corner of my eye as the light came up."

Gilbert's voice cracked and he swallowed hard. His eyes moistened but no tears fell.

"Sorry," he whispered, returning to his head and chin stroking.

"That's ok, sir. Take your time. It's not every day this sort of thing happens to you."

Stark let the guy compose himself, then continued.

"What did you do once you noticed her?"

"I went over an' had a look. I could tell she was dead, so I called 999 an' waited for you guys to get here, eh."

"You didn't notice anything else, anything suspicious?"

"Naw, I don't think so. What like?" replied Gilbert.

"Oh, I don't know. If you didn't notice anything, that's fine. Was there anyone else around?" asked Stark.

Gilbert went back to stroking his chin. Stark was beginning to find it irritating. He wanted to tell the scruffy bugger to go down the barber's and get a shave – face and head.

"Naw, I didn't see anyone else. I never usually do that early in the morning, eh. That's one of the reasons I like it so much. It's quiet, there's no dogs running about, an' I get the place to myself."

"Fair enough. Is there anything else you want to tell me, Mr Gilbert?"

He shrugged again and shook his head, "Don't think so, no."

"Ok, thanks. Can you pop into the station in Alloa as soon as you can an' we'll get an official statement from you?"

Gilbert nodded, "Ok, will do. I'll just go down the now. I'm no' working the day, so I'd rather get it over an' done with, eh."

"Sorry, can I just check: you didn't touch the girl did you?"

Gilbert looked horrified and affronted.

"No, I bloody well did not!" he said.

"That's fine, Mr Gilbert," said Stark, noticing the DCI clambering back over the broken distillery wall. "People do some funny things when they're in shock. However, I'll need you to submit a sample of DNA when you get to the station. It's standard practice in these situations."

"Right, aye. Ok," muttered Gilbert; uncertain but appeased, for now.

"If I need to talk to you again, Mr Gilbert, I'll give you a bell," said Stark.

The gangly, unkempt birder walked off towards his car, sparking up another cigarette as he went.

Stark and Barr went over to McLaren, who was sitting waiting for them in his car. He opened the window as they approached.

"So, what do you think?" asked the DCI.

Stark and Barr both made non-committal gestures.

"Nothing too suspicious so far, sir," replied Stark. "Says he was just down here watching birds when he found her. He seemed genuinely shocked. I think he's telling the truth. Have they fished her out yet?"

"Aye, no obvious signs of violence but we'll know more once they've done the post-mortem. No ID on her, so we've no name or address yet. What are you two doing now?"

"I was thinking we should go and check out the bridges, sir. No guarantee she jumped from one of them but, if she did, there might be something there."

"Aye, and we can't rule out the possibility she was pushed either, sir," chipped in Barr.

McLaren raised an eyebrow, "No, I don't suppose we can but let's hope that's no' the case, eh."

For once, Stark agreed with his irritating superior officer.

The newer of the two bridges, the Clackmannanshire Bridge was an interesting structure: a scalloped concrete platform, supported by a row of Y-shaped columns. Unlike most bridges of similar length, it didn't have any masts or cables suspended above the main deck; an attempt to minimise the effect it might have on migrating birds. It carried three lanes of traffic across its near one mile length – two leaving Clackmannanshire and one entering. Stark wondered if this was intended to send a subliminal message to the citizens of the Wee County. A guard rail flanked both sides: grey metal mesh stretched across four horizontal, parallel beams, supported by hundreds of triangular concrete posts. On the western side, a footpath allowed pedestrians to cross. Stark and Barr parked in a lay-by and walked out across the pathway, looking for anything out of the ordinary.

"First time I've been on here since it was built," said Stark.

"Me an' all, sir. Driven over it loads of times but never actually walked across it, eh."

"Are there any cameras on it?" asked Stark.

"No' sure, sir. Don't see anything obvious."

A stiff breeze ruffled the river below the bridge: brownish water flecked with white where the waves pinched the surface. Nothing about it said '*come on in!*'

Stark stopped, leant on the railings, and looked up river toward the jetty where the young girl had been found.

"If she did jump from here, there's a good chance nobody saw her do it. It's mid-morning and the traffic's pretty light. I imagine it's even quieter in the early hours."

"I would have thought so, sir. Also means if she didn't go swimming of her own accord, whoever helped her over the side wouldn't be seen either."

Stark cocked his head to the side and gave Barr a slight smile. His colleague wasn't giving up on his option of possible foul play.

"Aye, right enough, Ian. Can you get a bus to here?"

"I wouldn't think so, sir. Didn't see any stops."

"Why no car parked nearby, then? If she jumped, how did she get here?"

"Good point, sir. I'm sure that's what I was trying to tell you," said Barr, grinning.

Stark turned and looked back toward the Kincardine Bridge. A much shorter affair, it was designed to swing open to allow large ships passage up-river to the once-thriving port of Alloa. Since the demise of most of the heavy industries that used the port, it rarely needed to be opened any more. It was covered by cameras, looked to be carrying more traffic, and seemed far less suitable as a place for either suicide or murder.

"Let's go over to the other bridge and have a look, Ian. I don't think it's all that likely but best to cover all our options the now, eh. Just in case."

"Right you are, sir."
The two men headed back to their car.

3.

The ball smashed into the top corner of the net and the home crowd went wild – all three hundred and twenty-five of them. Paul Jacobs wheeled away, pointing to the name on the back of his shirt with both thumbs, slapping his chest with the palm of his hand, waiting to be swamped by gleeful team-mates. As good as the goal undoubtedly was, they didn't feel inclined to celebrate with as much enthusiasm as him. Screamer or not, they were still three goals behind with only a couple of minutes left on the clock and, with this being the last game of a record-breaking season in terms of poor performances, it hardly seemed worth the bother. Not only that but, as far as his cohorts were concerned, Jacobs could do without the encouragement.

A lone voice cut through the rain as he stood there basking in the adulation of his fans, "Fuck off Jacobs, you're no' playing in the Champion's League, eh. Nobody gies a fuck who you are, you wee diddy!" Laughter, a few more disparaging remarks, and a barrage of hand gestures inferring a fondness for pleasuring himself, accompanied this damning appraisal of his talents. Such were the joys of playing in the lowest of Scotland's senior football leagues. Jacobs should have kept his counsel, taken this abuse on the chin, but he couldn't. That was his fifteenth goal of the season. He'd scored more goals than the rest of the team put together. Without him, they'd be in an even worse position than they already were. All season he'd endured this kind of pish from these ungrateful wretches and something just snapped. As he ran back to the halfway line, he flicked the fans the bird. As ideas go, he'd had better.

Barry 'Baz' McGregor lacked many things, but a temper was not one of them. Performances on the pitch were insult enough and he wasn't taking that kind of crap from one of the inept clowns responsible for his discontent. He ran down the terracing steps, leapt over the advertising boards that flanked the pitch and barrelled toward Jacobs. At six foot three in height and nineteen stones in weight, he dwarfed Jacobs. However, what the footballer lacked in stature, he more than made up for in superior reflexes, a nice turn of speed and footwear designed to aid grip on a wet playing surface. As the infuriated giant bore down, ready to crush the life from him, Jacobs jinked to the side and dodged away from Baz, who sprawled full-length on the grass, cutting a muddy furrow as he went. A cheer went up from the crowd as he fell. This multiplied his rage exponentially. He tried to get up and slipped again. Another cheer. More rage. A couple of stewards in their high-visibility rain coats ran on to try and escort him from the pitch but they too fell foul of the underfoot conditions, going down in a heap. More cheers. This pantomime continued for a few minutes but, eventually, the stewards (and some reinforcements) managed to manhandle Baz away and wait for the police to come and cart him off to the cells to cool down.

The referee got the game back under way and, straight from the kick-off, the home team went 5-1 down. Boos rang out as the long-suffering support made for the exits. They may have been small in number but they were committed and passionate – losing hurt them and this season they'd taken a battering. Paul Jacobs was hurting too. Standing with hands on hips, he wondered what he was doing playing at this level of football, with these useless donkeys for team-mates; he was far better than this. That mouthy twat in the crowd hit a raw nerve. He needed to light a fire under his agent and get the hell out of Dodge.

"You know what, PJ, that guy in the crowd was right – you are a wee diddy!"

Tension in the dressing room had been mounting since the team trooped off in the rain and made for the tepid showers and basic changing facilities on offer. Frank Dawson; captain, senior player and all-round hard man of the team, saw the gesture Jacobs made and felt like finishing the job Baz McGregor started.

"Aye, right, Frank. Piss off! At least I'm no' a bitter, old has-been, playing out his days in this shitey wee league, knowing this is the best it's ever going to get. Actually, best it's ever been. You're just jealous coz you know I'm going places you never have and never will!"

For the second time that afternoon, Paul Jacobs provoked a reaction from his audience. Dawson lunged but, once again, Jacobs could thank his reflexes and speed for a side-step any professional boxer would have been proud of. Unfortunately for Frank Dawson, he didn't possess such innate abilities and, as he swiped at thin air, he lost his footing on the wet floor and went down. His left leg folded underneath him with a sickening crunch. A chorus of varying exclamations escaped the mouths of the team as Dawson bellowed in agony. Chaos erupted and Jacobs made good his escape.

By the time the ambulance drove off, with the sedated Dawson requiring emergency surgery, it was clear Paul Jacobs' wish to leave would be granted. Inadvertent or not, in prematurely ending the career of the club captain, he'd made his place in the team untenable. He should have been contrite; disappointed in himself; upset at what he'd done. Jacobs smiled as he sat in his car and pulled out his mobile phone. The caller ID told him it was Ali Muhammed, his agent.

"Ali, how's it going, my man?"

"Paul, what the hell's going on? I've had your manager on the phone to me demanding that I get you out of his club as soon as possible after you crippled his captain and goaded some guy in the crowd into attacking you. Is that right?"

"I don't give a shit about the Neanderthal that ran on the pitch, an' I don't give a shit about Frank Dawson either. The stupid old bastard got what he deserved. *He* attacked *me*. I'll tell you what, though, one thing the gaffer's definitely right about is that I'm getting out of there as soon as possible. It's time you started earning your fees, Ali. I'm better than this an' you know it. If you can't sort me out a move to a decent club, I'll find someone who can, eh."

Ali Muhammed dealt with a raft of football players. A lot of them were arrogant and difficult to handle but Jacobs trumped them all, especially since his own opinion of his talents was far in excess of anyone else's. He could sense a long, hot, uncomfortable summer coming up – regardless of the weather.

***

Jonny Jacobs lay on his bunk, hands behind his head, thinking. Today was his birthday. Fifty-five years old and celebrating – if that's what you could call it – behind bars. How had he let this happen? Years as a sporting hero, followed by years as a successful and respected publican, flushed down the crapper because he thought trusting that certified lunatic Malky McDuff was the way to resolve his financial issues. He swung his legs around and sat up, flexing his toes against the cold floor of his cell, hands gripping the edge of the bunk, head bowed.

This was the second year of his sentence for kidnapping Malky's little nephew Jack McDuff and demanding a ransom from his lottery-winning parents. Only six more to go.

Things had not gone well since his incarceration. Not long after he got there, a rumour began to circulate that Jonny Jacobs had interfered with the wee lad he'd kidnapped; that he was a nonce. Jonny knew who the source of the rumour was – the boy's father, Billy, serving a long sentence of his own for killing Malky. He might have been housed in a different prison, meaning he couldn't take direct action against Jonny himself, but Billy McDuff had plenty of connections inside. After a couple of severe beatings and a very unpleasant close-call involving a knife, Jonny had been moved into protective custody. He might well have been safer, but he was forced to mix with some of the least desirable human beings in Scotland. Worse still, they thought he was one of them, part of their vile club. A tear dropped onto the floor between his feet and he sniffed. He was sinking lower by the day. He really wanted a drink.

Visitors were rare. Only his younger brother, Sam, stood by him when he went down. Jonny was Sam's hero when they were growing up; his spell as a professional footballer cementing that status during his brother's late teens and early adulthood. One of the few things Jonny could still take pleasure in was the sporting achievements of Sam's son, Paul. The lad was talented – always had been. Before this catastrophe, Jonny used his contacts to get the boy noticed and signed up for a local club. Since he'd been in prison, Paul hadn't visited. It was fine. Jonny got it. The boy was in the public eye, a rising star. The last thing he needed was the kind of publicity visiting his jailbird uncle might bring. But it still hurt. Another tear plopped down on top of the previous one as Jonny stood up.

He heard a noise outside his door as something appeared from under it. He picked it up and felt a shudder of despair quake through him. The newspaper cutting showed his nephew raising a middle finger to the crowd after scoring a goal. The headline *'Jacobs Hits a Cracker then Takes the Biscuit'* wasn't what got to him. In the main body of the article, the journalist had written *'Paul Jacobs, nephew of convicted child kidnapper and former Alloa player, Jonny Jacobs ...*

' but someone had scored out '*kidnapper*' and written *rapist* above it in red pen. Jonny felt the frustration and anguish rise up in him. The room swam out of focus as a blind rage took hold. The paper was shredded as he slammed around his cell, sending personal chattels flying and breaking a couple of fitments. The noises he made were unlike anything any of his wardens had ever experienced before. After a brief skirmish, they managed to restrain him. However, with no sign of his fury or the torrent of nonsensical ranting abating, a doctor was called and a sedative administered.

Billy McDuff looked up from his bunk as Danny Weston stuck his head around the door frame, nodded and disappeared. Billy picked up the newspaper, tossed it into the bin at his bedside and smiled.

He made his way along to the telephones and dialled the number. Cammy answered within two rings.

"Alright, Da?"

"Aye, no' so bad son. How are you getting on?"

"Dodging away, Da, dodging away."

"Is everything sorted?"

"Getting there. Just a few loose ends to tie up, eh."

"Right, good. There's no way that bastard is getting away wi' what he did, eh."

"Naw, no way, Da. He'll get what's coming, don't worry about that."

"I'm no' worried, son. I've got all the time in the world, eh. We'll no' rush anything, we'll wait for the right moment an' do it right."

"Aye, of course. Sorry, Da, I've got to go. I'll speak to you later, eh."

"Aye, right you are, son. Cheers."

Billy McDuff put the phone back on its cradle and headed back to his cell. He would soon be rid of the itch he so badly needed scratched, and it felt good.

4.

Colin Cook felt uneasy and, therefore, a bit foolish. As a grown man, it made no sense for him to be spooked but something primal was gnawing at his nervous system. He normally welcomed the cooling properties of rain on such a long run, but it coated his glasses, impeding his vision. Most people would have tried contact lenses to solve this problem, but his world-class astigmatism meant this wasn't an option for him. He didn't really have the option to run without specs altogether as his unaided vision was so poor – especially in the dark – so rain-spattered glasses would have to do. He only wore a thin running vest and shorts, which were already sticking to his skin, so there was no point trying to dry the lenses with either of those. Even if rain-obscured correction was better than nothing at all; it didn't help reassure him to be left at such a disadvantage visually. The breeze slithered around his lean frame as he glanced at his watch and picked up the pace. He laughed at himself for being such a sap as the slick tarmac swept by under his quickening feet.

Colin was a strong runner. A schools' champion, he was once tipped to run for Team GB, before a persistent ankle problem stopped him training at the levels of intensity an elite athlete is required to maintain. As long as he didn't overdo it, he was fine to get out and pound the pavements two or three times a week without suffering any grave consequences. Running provided time to think; a bit of breathing space from the stresses and strains of the day and a welcome shot of endorphins. It also kept him fit and fended off any feelings of guilt in regard to the weekend blow-outs he and his mates were so fond of. He was lucky that his natural metabolic rate also helped to reduce his chances of taking up a career as a Sumo wrestler any time soon.

He liked to run this route, doing so on the majority of nights he ventured out. About seven miles in total, it mostly consisted of familiar, quiet, country lanes and didn't involve too many steep inclines. The trees lining the lane swayed and bowed as the wind encouraged them to take part in a sort of arboreal homage to the heavens. The rain pattered through the burgeoning canopy of leaves, a sudden increase in its intensity causing the drops that reached the ground to bounce up a few centimetres. This was no longer a pleasant evening run in the rain, it was a disconcerting slog in a downpour and a gale.

Colin glanced over his shoulder and saw the lights just in time. He dodged onto the grassy verge at the side of the road as the car swept past, sending a tsunami of puddle water crashing over him. The shock of the impact caused him to lose his footing and stumble. He felt searing pain shoot from his ankle to his hip as he swallow-dived and connected face-first with the ground. Once he'd slithered to a halt, he pushed himself up onto all fours, spitting out the vile concoction of mud and grass he'd just inadvertently ingested. He roared in pain as his old injury announced an agonising reprise, then turned his ire on the driver.

"You fucking bastard!" he shouted, extending the last word to the point of causing his voice to crack, such was the force and fervour with which he delivered it.

He'd lost his glasses in the fall, but he could make out the car's tail-lights further up the lane. It looked like it had stopped. Grimacing from the pain in his ankle, he started to feel around for his glasses in the immediate vicinity of where he'd landed, cursing constantly under his breath as to the injustice of it all and what he might do if he got hold of the inconsiderate shit who'd just floored him. He looked up again as the red dots on the back of the car dimmed. He heard the clunk of the door. Maybe the driver had a conscience after all and was coming back to make sure he was ok. Either that or they'd taken exception to Colin's character assassination and wanted to have it out with him. He'd rather it was the former. Minus his glasses and with only one functioning leg, it would be a thoroughly miserable journey home if they didn't offer him a lift. Worse still, if they fancied a scrap.

Colin could make out the form of somebody walking towards him. He didn't look all that tall and seemed to be dressed in dark clothing, but discerning much more detail through the rain and darkness wasn't easy. He kept feeling about for his glasses but wasn't having any luck. The driver stopped about twenty metres away from him.

"Alright, mate, can you help me, please? I lost my specs when I fell an' I canny see a thing now. I've hurt my ankle as well, an' it's bloody agony, eh," said Colin, trying to adopt a friendly tone, suppressing his irritation with the guy for having caused his trouble in the first place.

The stranger didn't reply and Colin felt a chill tinkle in his bones. The disquiet he'd felt before returned, only amplified. Scrabbling about on the ground in a vest and shorts, half-blinded and in pain, he suddenly felt vulnerable, compromised. The hair on the back of his neck bristled.

"Sorry, have you got a phone, mate? It would be great if you could maybe phone my dad for me. He could come and get me. Or maybe you could give me a lift, eh? I don't think I can walk," he said, trying again to elicit a response.

Nothing.

As the rain cascaded down, the heat he'd produced by running radiated into the night, leaving him shivering. He looked again at the silent figure, squinting, trying to pick out more detail. He was wearing a hooded rain jacket but he couldn't see any of his facial features. Definitely not tall or physically imposing; even with only one leg he fancied his chances, so why did he feel so unnerved? Something about him was familiar and yet not.

"Look, mate, if you're no' going to help, then just piss off. If you'd been paying more attention, I wouldn't be in this mess, eh." He decided to try bravado, given that polite and jovial had failed to garner any kind of response. He wasn't going to let this little shitbag intimidate him.

Colin tried to stand but regretted it. The pain almost caused him to black out and he sat down again, clutching at his ankle, giving out a long, low exclamation as to how much discomfort it was causing him.

Still the stranger stood, unmoving, silent; the rain sheeting down; the wind unabated.

"What's your fuckin problem, mate? You deaf? I told you to piss off if you're no' going to help, now do one!" shouted Colin. His bravado wavered, causing his voice to wobble.

The mute stranger began to walk away.

"Aye, good! On your fuckin way, pal! I'll be fine, you utter prick. You practically run me over, then you come back an' just stand there instead of helping. It's no' me that needs help, mate, it's you, you fuckin psycho!" he shouted after the retreating figure.

The driver didn't look back, didn't respond. Colin heard the door of the car close and saw the tail-lights move off and away out of sight. He put his hand down to his side. His fingers brushed against the leg of his glasses. They were more or less intact; a little bent but he put them on and could see again. It was a minor victory. The shivering increased and he made a second attempt to stand. Again agonising pain thwarted him.

As he sat on the verge, soaking, freezing, in agony; his emotions cracked. He wept in self-pity and remorse. Whenever anything bad happened to him, he remembered, and he felt the finger of karma tapping him on the shoulder. He was sorry, he really was.

So sorry.

So very sorry.

5.

Stark regarded himself as a strong person; an optimist, someone who'd been kicked to the ground by life more than most but always managed to get up, dust himself off and keep on going. At least, that's what he used to think.

The amber liquid in his glass rotated gently as he made small circles with his wrist. He took another mouthful and placed the glass down on the table. There it joined the half-empty bottle that would replenish it, a couple of take-away cartons from the Chinese, one plate, one fork and one knife. He swallowed, savouring the whisky's delicate sweetness followed by its fiery nip. He looked around the living room in the bungalow he'd inherited from his mother and felt the weight of loneliness bearing down on him.

Years of living away from Alloa had left him short of any real connections in the town. One old friend was married with a couple of kids. A recent drinking session revealed they no longer had anything much in common. The exercise had not been repeated. His only other old pal who still lived in the town was Tommo Shaw. But he worked the rigs and when he wasn't working, he was living the high life his inflated salary afforded him. They'd spoken on the phone a couple of times and exchanged texts but their oft-mooted reunion drink had never materialised. His colleague and subordinate Ian Barr used to be an option for socialising. However, after years of trying and failing to impregnate his wife, he appeared to have developed the virility of a rabbit. One baby was already in situ and, less than six months after its miraculous appearance, another was on the way. Needless to say, Barr's free time was at a premium. Free time he was permitted to spend getting bladdered with his boss dried up completely.

Stark stood and walked over to the couch, picked up the remote and switched on the television. Game shows, a costume drama, reality programmes, a film he'd seen more than once, a film he watched only a couple of nights previously, shopping channels, a history programme, more reality shite, property, antiques, more reality shite, re-runs of *Top Gear,* a US cop show that required more concentration than a half-cut man could give it. He switched it off and dropped the remote.

The laptop sat on the arm of the couch, a light blinking to indicate he'd forgotten to switch it off before closing the lid. He picked it up, took it over to the table, cleared a space and opened it up. He hit the space bar and the internet browser sprung to life. The battery didn't look too low, so he could do without the power cable for now, which was just as well because it was through the back of the house somewhere and he couldn't be arsed going to get it. He started to surf.

Stark checked a few football related items on the BBC, watched a YouTube video of *Radiohead* at Glastonbury, and had a look at what Amazon were recommending for him. As it happened, they failed to pique his interest much or open his wallet. Social media wasn't his thing. He didn't have Facebook or Twitter accounts. To be honest, in his line of work, they were a liability. Too many cops had been caught out by posting material deemed 'inappropriate' by their employer. For similar reasons, Stark avoided watching porn on his own computer. Careers had also been left in tatters thanks to careless meanderings into that seedy world. He went back to the BBC home page.

Stark recharged his glass and took another belt of whisky. As he sat there, feeling the alcohol take effect on him, numbing nerve endings, dulling thought processes, he noticed a headline about online dating. An unfamiliar tightness in his gut pulled his attention toward it. The cursor hovered on the link but something stopped him clicking. This was stupid, pathetic even. A few too many drinks, a night on his own and he was turning into some sort of sad, desperate, lonely heart. He clicked.

The article presented all sorts of statistics about how many folks used these services nowadays. Case studies involving happy people with shiny new partners accompanied quotes from psychologists, counsellors and industry figures. Fascinating as it all was, he wouldn't be going down that route just yet. He might be Billy-No-Mates but he could still get a woman by more traditional means – if he wanted to.

He shut down the computer, drained his glass and took it and the bottle across to the coffee table. Slumping onto the couch, he poured another large one, switched on the television again, turned to the film he'd watched a few night's previously and channel-hopped endlessly until his eyes drooped. It wasn't long before he nodded off, glass in one hand, remote in the other and television still on.

***

Duncan Cook sat in his armchair watching a film he'd only just watched a couple of nights ago; best of a bad bunch. He glanced up at the clock on his mantelpiece and wondered if he'd somehow missed his son returning from an evening run. He got up and walked through to the hallway. No running shoes by the door where the lazy bastard usually left them to form a puddle that his mother would clear up without challenging him about it. She really was too soft on the boy – always had been. Boy! That was a joke; he was twenty three years old. A man, earning his own wage and should be more than capable of tidying away after himself. On the off-chance that miracles do happen, and the boy had decided to break with indolent tradition, he checked the cupboard under the stairs. Still no running shoes. Anxiety prickled across his skin.

He went upstairs and looked into the boy's bedroom. Empty. His unease increased. Next, he went to the window and checked the driveway. The lad's car was still there and it was sheeting down. It looked quite windy too. Now, he was properly worried. He wondered if he should alert his wife to the situation but decided against it. He could see she'd already switched off her bedside light and was likely asleep. Margo preferred to go to bed early and rise early; he was more of a night owl. There was no need to worry her at this point. There was bound to be a logical explanation for why Colin hadn't come home yet.

Duncan went downstairs, put on shoes and a coat, grabbed his car keys and quietly slipped out of the house. He knew the route his son usually took when he went out running. His heart thumped in his chest and nausea sloshed in his gut as his imagination began to run away with itself. He got in the car and drove out into the night.

6.

The chime of a text alert woke Stark. He wished it hadn't. His tongue felt like he'd spent the whole of the previous evening using it to clean the carpet and his gut seemed to be touting itself as an ideal replacement for his washing machine. The text was from Ian Barr.

Hi sir, can u call me please? Cheers, Ian.

Stark struggled to his feet, head like a bowling ball. It was seven thirty. He must have slept on the couch for about eight hours but it didn't feel like it. Stiffness and hangover combined to ensure he made straight for a shower.

Suitably refreshed and waiting for the kettle to boil, Stark called Barr.

"Ian, what's happening?"

"Alright, sir, yeah, the boss put out an appeal last night about the river girl and we've had a possible positive response this morning."

"Really?"

"Aye, the guy's coming into the station this morning an' the boss says you've to interview him, eh."

Stark let out a sigh. "I'm supposed to be on a back shift. Can you no' do it, Ian?"

"I offered, eh, but the DCI says the guy's a local big-wig and he'll expect to be dealt wi' by somebody more senior than me."

"If that's the case, how come the DCI isn't doing it himself?"

"Don't know, sir, sorry. He just told me to get you, so that's what I'm doing."

"Who is this local big-wig anyway?" asked Stark.

"Grant Cook; runs Cook Brothers Building Services.

Him and his brother, Duncan, also own Cook Haulage, eh."

"Oh, great, no doubt that means it's got something to do wi' rolled up trouser legs an' funny handshakes. What time is Cook due in?"

"Nine o'clock."

"Right, I'll see you then. Cheers, Ian."

"Ok, sir, see you in a bit."

Stark switched on the radio in the kitchen as he made his tea and toast. The local bulletin contained a piece about the girl right enough. DCI Don McLaren gave a minimal account of the discovery of the body while asking for public help regarding her identity. Stark took a couple of paracetamol and sipped at his tea. He had hoped to go and have a look for a new car that morning before starting his shift, but that would need to wait.

He sat down at the kitchen table and used his phone to look for info on the Cooks. He knew of the companies – their trucks had rumbled around the local area since he was a boy and numerous building projects had displayed their company livery over the years. He didn't know much about the brothers who owned them, though.

From their photographs, Stark would have said the Cook brothers were in their fifties. The company biography on their website told of how their father had started the haulage firm in the mid-1970's. In the 1980's they all started the building business together and, despite a couple of difficult recessions, both businesses were still going strong. The father died in 1995 and since then the brothers had been in charge. Both men liked to highlight how much they gave to local charities and it was obvious they played a prominent role in local politics – hardly surprising given how dependent half their business was on planning permissions. Stark was going to look at some other search results but, realising the time, closed down the phone and got on his way. He could do without starting the day by falling out with McLaren for keeping his VIP waiting.

Grant Cook had the appearance of a troubled man. Grey stubble bristled across his face, his shock of grey-white hair had not made the acquaintance of a comb that morning, dark circles smudged the skin under his eyes and his clothing had a dishevelled, slept-in kind of look to it. In fact, he made Stark look good in comparison. He stood as Stark entered the interview room and extended his hand.

"Grant Cook. You DI Stark?" he asked in a gruff local accent untouched by years of rubbing shoulders with the business elite of Scotland.

"That's me," replied Stark, shaking his hand. Like the accent, Cook retained the monstrous, calloused paws of a man accustomed to hard, physical graft. A sturdy, solid-looking man but not what you'd call overweight, with a weathered complexion; Stark imagined he'd be a fearsome guy to get on the wrong side of.

"Good, DCI McLaren told me you were his best man."

As the two men sat down at the table in the middle of the room, Stark couldn't help but feel aggrieved by the obvious, convenient half-truth told by McLaren. Recent cutbacks following the merger of the various Scottish police divisions meant their staffing levels had taken a bit of a beating and Stark was now the most senior officer based in Alloa, McLaren apart. In truth, he was McLaren's only option. The DCI would never have given Stark such a glowing compliment first-hand. Stark wondered again why McLaren didn't deal with Cook himself if they were old pals. Maybe they weren't pals at all? Maybe this was just McLaren playing politics with an influential local? Then again, it might be he just bottled being the bearer of bad news.

"So, I understand you have some concerns about your daughter, Mr Cook," said Stark.

Cook wrung his hands, a haunted look passing over his face as he took Stark's gaze, "I think the lassie you found in the Forth might be," he choked with emotion, trying not to let any tears fall, "might be my Debbie."

"Ok, I know this is hard for you, Mr Cook, but can you tell me why you think the girl we found might be your daughter?"

The hand-wringing continued and Cook took a couple of deep breaths before continuing. "My daughter's a student at Stirling Uni. She's a typical youngster; got a mobile, Facebook, all that stuff. We don't see her every day but most days we get a call, a text or see some kind of update online, eh. It dawned on me yesterday that we'd no' heard anything from her for a couple of days. Her mobile just goes through to voicemail an' she's no' replied to any texts. My wife went online to check but there was nothing new since Tuesday. I phoned one of her pals but they'd no' heard anything either. That's when I started worrying, like."

He stopped to take a sip of water and compose himself again.

"Anyway, I went round her flat last night an' there was no answer. I've got a key, so I let myself in an' she wasn't there. Then I heard the news report an' I got a very bad feeling. I called up this morning an' arranged to come an' see you, so here I am."

Stark looked up from his notes. "I take it this is out of character for Debbie?"

"Definitely. We've never gone without contact for this long before. She's a good kid." He choked back his emotions again. "She's very close to her Mam, it's just no' like her at all, eh."

"Did you bring a photograph of Debbie with you, Mr Cook?"

Cook fished inside his jacket and pulled out a photo. "Aye, here you go."

Stark looked at the image of the smiling, long-haired blonde and tried not to react. This was the girl they'd pulled from the river. He'd been to see the body the day before and this was definitely her. He needed to go as gently as he could.

"Ok, I'm afraid you need to prepare yourself for some bad news, Mr Cook."

A shudder went through the man and he seemed to shrink away in front of Stark's eyes.

"Oh no! Oh, fuckin hell, Debbie. No, no, no!"

"I'm very sorry, Mr Cook, but I think the girl we pulled from the river is indeed your daughter, Debbie. I'll need you to complete a formal identification. Do you think you'll be able to do that today?"

Cook looked up, tears running down his face and nodded. "I want to go now. I need to see her. I need to be sure it's her."

Stark nodded and stood up. "If you'd like to follow me, sir, I'll arrange for a car to take us down to the mortuary."

Cook got up and trudged out the door. A man used to being as strong as the steel, concrete and bricks he worked with, reduced to emotional rubble.

"Turned out it was her right enough, sir," said Stark.

DCI McLaren stood looking out the window of his office. It wasn't much of a view and he wasn't really looking at anything in particular.

"Shit, that's no' good. Have we had the post-mortem report in yet?"

"She drowned, sir. No signs of a struggle, no sexual assault involved, no signs of any injuries other than minor abrasions, consistent with being dragged along the bottom of a river by the current. Toxicology showed traces of tamazepam in her blood."

McLaren turned to face Stark. "How did Grant Cook take it?"

"No' too good, sir. Understandable really, she was an only child. But I suppose you knew that?"

McLaren frowned. "How would I have known that, eh?"

Stark was a bit surprised. "Oh, sorry, sir, I thought you knew him."

"I know *of* him, Stark, but I don't know him personally."

"Right, fair enough, sir. Anyway, looks like a suicide after all. Although, when I mentioned this to Cook, he was adamant that was impossible, that his daughter would never have killed herself."

"No parent likes to hear that sort of thing though, eh," said McLaren. "I don't know how I'd handle something like that if she was mine. He's bound to be unwilling to accept the truth right now."

Stark found himself transported back to his mother's kitchen in the aftermath of Carrie's death; his parents bereft, his own emotions churning and raw. The anger, the bewilderment, but most of all the impotence. He snapped back into the moment.

"Agreed. So, do you want me to do anything more about it, sir, or just write it up as suicide an' move on?" asked Stark.

McLaren looked pensive, uncertain. He turned to look out of the window again.

"It's a tricky one, Stark. Grant Cook's a well-connected guy, eh. He holds a lot of sway in the top circles. It might be a good idea for us to humour him, do a bit of cursory investigation; satisfy him we did something for him in his hour of need. You ken what I mean?"

Stark nodded. That answered the question of why Stark had been dragged in to talk to Cook. "Aye, no bother, sir. I'll do a few interviews, try an' gather enough evidence from friends an' that regarding her mental state to confirm suicide as most likely."

"Aye, that'll be fine, Stark. But don't go blowing a load of the budget on this, eh. Things are getting pretty hairy around here financially since the reshuffle. Last thing I need is a bollocking from the Chief Super for overspending, right?"

"No problem, sir," said Stark and walked out of the office.

The identification had not been pleasant. Cook collapsed when he saw his daughter, weeping uncontrollably and needing Stark's help to get back on his feet. The reaction to Stark's suggestion that his daughter probably killed herself was so vehement, he thought Cook might get physical with him for suggesting it. It was a horrible thing but, as difficult as it was for the businessman to accept, Stark was pretty sure she'd ended up in the river without anyone else's encouragement. It might have been a tragic accident; a superficial relief to her parents, no doubt, but nothing he could do was going to make Grant Cook feel any better.

**

Colin Cook's head spun. It felt as if his sense of himself was being washed down a plughole. Debbie was dead. His closest ally. The one he could always turn to when it all got too much. One of the few who understood, who was there. Numbness spread through him – it felt as if someone had slipped him an anaesthetic while he wasn't looking. He thought he should be crying but no tears would flow.

The phone buzzed. Paul Jacobs. Colin answered like an automaton.

"Hello."

"Coco? It's Paul. I just heard, mate. I don't really know what to say."

"Alright, Paul. It's just a fuckin nightmare, I can't believe she's dead, eh."

"I hear you, bro'. I'm struggling to get my head round it. What happened? Do you know?"

"I … it's … well, that's the worst bit about it. The police reckon she killed herself."

Silence roared between them for a few seconds.

"Oh, fuck. That's horrendous. Are they sure? I would never have Debbie down as suicidal," said Jacobs.

"Me neither. I can't take it in, eh. It's such a waste. I mean, if she was having bother, why didn't she speak to me? I could have helped her, you know?"

"Definitely, mate. Definitely."

Another silence grew. This one less aggressive, more foetid.

"You don't think it was anything to do with … " said Jacobs.

Colin cut across him. "Don't, Paul. Just don't. I've got enough fucked-up thoughts in my head. I don't need any more, eh."

"Alright, no worries, Coco, mate. Look, I'm going to go. I'll be round later, take you out for a drink. Have a proper chat. Ok?"

"Ok. See you later."

Colin cancelled the call and sat down heavily on his bed.

Sorry.

So very sorry.

7.

The Cook's house was suitably palatial; an impressive shop window for their business. It stood alone on the top of a ridge that provided magnificent views. The enormous garden swept out and around it; the neat lawns running up to meet woods and fields on all sides. The stone-chip driveway fanned out in front of the house, providing space for numerous cars to park. Grant Cook appeared to like cars. A Bentley, a Range Rover and a convertible Mini Cooper adorned this area in front of the house. They made Stark's beat-up Ford Focus look like a weed in a flowerbed.

Anne Cook answered the door looking red-eyed, drawn and haggard; exactly how most recently-bereaved parents looked in Stark's experience. Despite the mask of grief distorting her features, she was a good-looking woman and her likeness to Debbie was striking.

He held up his warrant card. "Hello, Mrs Cook. I'm DI Adam Stark. I arranged with Mr Cook to come over and speak to you both about Debbie."

She nodded, her lip trembling and any intended words of greeting failing to get beyond her throat. Opening the door wide, she motioned for him to enter.

The large entrance hallway was dominated by a huge staircase and a spectacular chandelier; pure crystal, no doubt. Anne Cook led him across polished wooden floors, along a passageway to the back of the house, through the kitchen and into a huge conservatory. Grant Cook stood as Stark entered and walked towards him to shake hands.

"Hi DI Stark, thanks for coming over. Do you want a cup of tea?"

"Well, don't go to any bother, but if you're having one

anyway, then I will too," replied Stark.

"It's no bother," whispered Anne before heading back to the kitchen.

"Come and sit down, mate," said Grant, gesturing towards a large, white leather sofa.

Stark sat and sank deep into the cowhide. It was the most luxurious thing he'd ever planked his buttocks on in his life.

"You've got a beautiful house, Mr Cook."

"Aye, thanks. Built it myself. Been here ten years. No' sure we'll be able to stay now though, eh. After what's happened." The sentence hung in the air like a bad smell before Cook cleared his throat and continued. "Oh, an' call me Grant, will you? No need to be so formal."

"Right, no bother," replied Stark.

A little more small talk passed between them about the cars and gardening before Anne returned with a tray and the tea. She looked like she'd been crying again. Once they were settled and drinks allocated, Stark began to ask the Cooks some questions.

"I realise this is a terrible time for you both but we need to just make sure we've no' missed anything, ok?"

They both nodded.

"I'm sorry it upset you so much when we spoke before, Mr Cook – sorry, Grant – but, I have to be completely honest with you and say that all the evidence so far is suggesting that your daughter took her own life."

Anne Cook crumpled, shaking and sobbing. Grant put his arm around her and looked at Stark with a more resigned expression than the near-violent indignation he displayed in the mortuary.

"We know that, son, but we just can't accept it without being sure. We need to rule out anything else an' we want to know why. That's all the matters to us now. Why."

Stark let Anne Cook recover her composure.

"Did you notice anything unusual about Debbie's mood or behaviour in the run up to her going missing?"

They both shook their heads.

"Naw, nothing."

"She didn't seem depressed or down about anything?"

Again they responded in the negative.

"Was Debbie in a relationship?"

"I don't think so," said Anne. "Nothing serious, at least, or important enough to share with me."

"Grant said you were close. I take it she'd definitely have told you if she was?"

She barely managed to make her reply audible. "Yes."

"How about friends, did she have any particularly close friends?"

"She had lots of friends. She was always popular – she was Head Girl in her final year at school," said Grant.

"Right, do you have the contact details for any of them?" asked Stark.

"Well, we could probably get them for a few of her friends that we know well an' that still stay round here, but there's going to be loads of Uni ones we've no' met, eh," said Grant, a weary look casting a shadow over his features.

"Aye, that's ok. I imagine, like most youngsters now, she'd use her phone to keep in touch, rather than having a paper address book?"

"I'd have thought so, aye."

"Unfortunately, it looks like her phone was lost in the river so, unless we manage to recover it, we're going to have to try an' find some other way of getting in touch wi' her pals an' so on," said Stark, pausing before continuing with his questioning. "You run your businesses in partnership with your brother, Duncan. Is that right?"

"Aye."

"Would it be ok if I went to speak to him as well?"

"Of course. Duncan and Margo were really close to her too. They just want to know why an' all," said Grant.

"Do they have any kids?"

"They've got a laddie, Colin, our nephew. He was more

like a brother than a cousin to Debbie when they were growing up. We stayed next door to each other for years, eh. Made running the business a lot easier, apart from anything else."

Stark made some notes.

"It would be great if you could let your friends and family know we're looking for information, for help in finding out more about Debbie's movements and mood in the past few weeks. Is that ok?"

"Aye, we can do that, son," replied Grant, "they'll all be happy to help us try an' find out what went so wrong for our wee lassie that she needed to … " Grant didn't finish the sentence, his voice fizzling out as he tried.

Stark stood up.

"Do you think I could have a look in Debbie's room?"

"Why?" asked Anne Cook, all of a sudden animated and anxious.

"It's standard practice, Mrs Cook. Have you been in there since you received your bad news?"

"Yes, but I couldn't stay long. I don't want you to touch anything. You understand?"

Stark had seen this happen so many times. It was a classic reaction to loss. "Don't worry, Mrs Cook, I understand how hard this must be. I'll be very careful and I promise not to remove anything without your permission."

"How would you know what it's like? You've not got a clue how I feel!"

"Actually, Mrs Cook, I think I do know. My own sister killed herself a few years ago and I know exactly what you're going through."

The Cooks both looked shocked at this revelation.

"Oh, god, I'm sorry. It's just … I can't …" she said, then stood and walked out of the conservatory and off down the garden.

"It's ok, son. Don't worry about it. I'll take you up there," said Grant, standing and gesturing for Stark to go ahead of him.

They climbed the huge staircase, with its beautiful deep-pile carpet, up to the landing and then on to the bedroom. Stark put on a pair of gloves and went into the room. His shattered chaperone leant on the door frame, keeping watch over him.

It was very tidy. The bed made, nothing cluttering the floor, books neatly arranged on a shelving unit, a few CD's stacked alongside a compact music system. It was then he remembered that Debbie didn't live there – she had her own flat. He opened a few drawers, looked in the almost empty wardrobe and checked under the four-poster bed. Nothing seemed out of place and, there was no diary, note or any other written materials as far as he could tell. If she had kept a diary or written a suicide note, they would likely be in the flat. Something did catch his eye as he was about to finish up: a set of artworks all depicting water. One striking charcoal sketch stood out from the others. It depicted a broiling, dark sea, with some kind of monster rearing up from it in silhouette. They were all initialled DAC and dated from 2012 up to the current year.

"Did Debbie do all of these herself?" he asked.

"Aye, she's very creative. She wanted to go to Art School at one point but decided to do Film and Media instead. I always found it odd she chose to paint water so much as she hated it – never learnt to swim ..."

The significance of this was not lost on either man, and Stark waited for a moment to allow the emotion it produced to subside before continuing.

"When did Debbie last stay here, Grant?"

Cook scratched at his head. "About a month ago. I think she likes being off the leash. Loves that flat. *Best thing ever*; that's what she told me when I gave her the keys." He looked away and let out a small sob. Stark noticed he'd talked about her in the present tense. It would take time for this to fade from Cook's language.

"Ok, I'm done here, Grant. I think I need to take a look in her flat, though. Can you get me a key an' give me the address, please?" Stark said as he came out of the room.

"Aye, let's go back down. I want to make sure Anne's alright. She's no' doing too good, eh. It's ripped her fuckin heart out … mine too."

Stark followed Grant Cook back downstairs, across a carpet worth more than his car and past a chandelier that may have cost as much as half his house, contemplating how little all this opulence and wealth would matter anymore to the people who'd accumulated it.

The state of the bedroom in Debbie Cook's flat contrasted sharply with the one in her parent's house. It was a shambles. The bed was unmade, expensive-looking clothes and shoes were scattered about, while various stationery items, piles of papers and text-books covered the desk. A laptop lay on the floor beside the bed. The dressing table was decorated with make-up, perfume, an empty bottle of wine and a lipstick-stained glass. The mirror had photos, postcards and magazine cuttings inserted all around its frame. It was just how a student bedroom should look. It reeked of freedom from parental interference and the carefree abandon of youth.

Grant Cook had insisted on leading Stark down here and letting him in. Stark suspected it was to appease his distraught wife, whom he'd spent some considerable time consoling before they left. Stark didn't mind.

"Sorry about the fuckin mess, eh," said Cook, looking a bit embarrassed.

"Naw, naw, this is fine. My bedroom looks worse than this," said Stark, trying to lighten the mood. It didn't have much effect.

Stark sifted through the books and papers on the desk but didn't find anything unusual. It all seemed to be related in some way to her University course. Stark knew it wasn't that likely she'd be keeping a diary – Facebook, Twitter and all that stuff meant, these days, most people blurted out a record of their feelings, thoughts and whereabouts publicly, rather than furtively or introspectively. He opened drawers and checked the wardrobe which, this time, was full to bursting.

There was no obvious note in the flat either. It didn't mean much in itself but it was commoner to have one than not. It could be on the computer but that seemed unlikely. More disappointing was the continuing lack of a mobile phone. Without that, they were going to waste a lot of time. The laptop might help a bit – especially if she'd synched her contacts onto it – but there were no guarantees she had.

"Oh, I meant to ask; did Debbie have a car, by any chance?"

"Naw. She never showed any interest in driving. I offered to pay for lessons but she wasn't bothered. Why?"

"Ach, you know, just in case there was somewhere else to look for clues."

This was a half-truth, concealing his concern about how Debbie had found her way onto the bridge. Depression, if she was suffering from it, could cause odd behaviour. She could have walked a long way to get there, but it just didn't seem that likely.

"I'm going to take this laptop away an' have someone check it over. I'll return it once we're done," Stark told Cook, looking to get off the subject of the car as quickly as he could.

"Ok, son. Whatever it takes. We just want some answers, eh. Look, Detective Stark, I wasn't totally up-front with you back at the house."

Stark frowned.

"Well, you asked if we'd noticed anything about Debbie's moods an' we said we'd no' seen anything unusual. That's no' strictly true. I just didn't want to say anything in front of Anne – she's having a hard enough time of it."

"Right," said Stark.

"Aye, well, Debbie was definitely no' herself the past couple of months. Since she started the new term at Uni. I just thought it was teething trouble, you know? New situation, living away for the first time, needing to fit in wi' a new crowd, eh."

"Yeah, I understand. So, what made you think that?"

"She was less cheery, less chatty, than usual. She wouldn't tell me anything. Kept saying it was nothing to worry about." Cook sucked in his breath and looked away. " I should have got her to talk to Anne."

Stark felt for the man. Cook was starting to blame himself. "Right, well, thanks for telling me that, Grant. I know it can't have been easy but it all helps paint a picture for us. Anyway, that's me finished here. I'll be back in touch soon."

The two men shook hands.

"You go on ahead, son. I'm going to stop here for a bit, eh. I just want a minute to myself, you ken what I mean?"

Stark nodded and walked out the front door. He knew just what the girl's grieving father meant; he could do with a minute to gather his own emotions.

Back at the station, Stark found Barr still working on reports. He put the computer down on the desk beside him.

"Alright, Ian. This is the laptop belonging to the Cook lassie. I need you to have a look through an' see what you can find out about what was going on in her life. See if there's any clues or reasons to explain why she might have killed herself."

"Right you are, sir."

"And, Ian?" said Stark as he walked across to his desk.

"Aye?"

"The parents are having a really hard time an' I promised the lassie's mother we'd be careful wi' her stuff. Right?"

"Ok, sir."

***

The bar was just a bar; nothing special, but not a dump either. Stark looked at his watch and noted that Tommo was now half an hour late. This was not unusual as far as he could recall – even if it had been a few years since they'd been out on the town together. Tommo was the friend who was always late, a bit of a flake, self-absorbed and unreliable. Tommo was the friend most people would inevitably drift apart from as they got older because he made maintaining any contact with him such a chore. Not a bad guy, just a frustrating one. But Stark felt compelled to make that effort, to at least try.

They first met, aged five, when they were thrown into the same class in first year of primary school. This ensured they had a shared history that spanned so many brilliant and terrible events in both their lives. Trying to get Tommo to appreciate their friendship as much as Stark appreciated it was a losing battle he fought every time they arranged to do something together. He couldn't seem to stop getting booted in the emotional scrotum, over and over. The archetypal triumph of hope over experience.

Two pints later, Stark's phone beeped.

Sorry mate. Been called back to the rigs early. Need to pack a bag and get my shit together. I'll catch up with you later. Cheers, Tommo.

Stark looked at the message, feeling the usual mixture of hurt, anger and impotence only his oldest friend could induce in him. It was probably true but he couldn't shake the feeling that Tommo was soft-soaping him; bottling out of what he really wanted to say, which was that he didn't want to go for a drink with Stark at all.

Ok mate. No bother. I'll see you later. Cheers, A

He hit send, put the phone back in his pocket and ordered another beer.

It was getting busy now. Couples, a few guys and then a group of about six women came in. Stark clocked the petite blonde right away. As she approached the bar to order some drinks he checked her ring finger – unadorned.

She was a stunner.

After she'd ordered a round of shots, their eyes met and she smiled. He reciprocated and she blushed. Not a full-on *red-neck* as they used to call them in school, just a hint of pink. She gathered up the shots and returned to her mates. It didn't take long before her turn came around again.

"You lot are going for it are you not?" he said. For once, the music in the bar didn't require them to bellow in each other's ears and demand umpteen repetitions to get the message across.

"Aye, my pal's pal got a new job yesterday, so we're having a wee knees-up to celebrate, eh," she replied, the blush flashing and fading across her pale skin again. Stark could detect the alcohol in her diction. She was getting quite pissed and he found it endearing, attractive even.

"Good for her. Do you know her well?" He needed to plant a seed if he wanted to split her from the pack, as women were rarely as mercenary in such situations as men would be.

"Eh, no' really. It's my pal, Emma, that I'm here with." She turned and pointed to a rather overweight girl with short black hair and thick-framed glasses. "I don't really know the other girls that well, but they seem nice."

"They like a bevvy, that's for sure," he said, laughing and touching her on her arm.

She laughed in response; a giggle that reeked of mischief and sexual promise. "Aye, they sure do. But, that's ok, coz so do I!"

They laughed together.

"Do you think you might be able to sneak off for a drink with me?" asked Stark, deciding to be bold.

She looked at him, then across to the table as she gathered up her shots, then back to him. "Eh, I … look, it's nice of you to offer. I'm flattered an' that but, don't take this the wrong way, I think you're a bit too old for me. Sorry."

Stark almost choked on the beer he'd just sipped and looked at her in disbelief. She made it to full red-neck status and walked away. He watched her pert little arse as it wiggled off and thought about what she'd just said. How much older than her was he? He looked over to the table. She'd put down the drinks and appeared to be explaining to Emma what had just happened. Laughter rocked around the group of women. Apart from the blonde, they all raised their glasses to him in a drunken, disparaging toast before slamming their shots back in one. Stark was mortified, affronted and apoplectic all at once. He got up and made for the door, trying not to look in the direction of the derision being hurled his way.

As he stepped into the street, the little blonde came out and grabbed his arm to stop him.

"I'm sorry about my pals, I didn't … " was all she managed before Stark cut her off.

"Whatever, hen. But, just as a matter of interest, how old are you?"

"I'm nineteen."

"Oh, for fuck's sake," he said as he walked away, heading for the station and a train home.

Stark looked at the form and let the cursor hover over the submit button. He felt daft, inadequate, embarrassed and weird in equal measure. There was a definite frisson of excitement weaving in and out of those feelings as well. Could he really do this? Did he need to do this? *I'm nineteen.* His finger pressed down and it was gone. He took a slug of whisky and flopped down on the couch, thinking about all sorts of things this might lead to.

It had been quite a night. Bombed out by his pal for being a boring old bastard, then bombed out by a teenage beauty queen for being a deluded, lecherous old bastard. He still smarted from the indignity of the knock back and the mass piss-take in the bar. He could never go back there again. How had this happened? How had he got so old so quickly, and why hadn't he even noticed? He was still the right side of forty but only just. He'd never considered that to be old until the blonde made it clear that she thought it was. He still had all his hair, even if it was beginning to show the first signs of thinning a tad, and there was no grey, so far. He wasn't overweight for a big guy – he could still button his five-year-old jeans and he could still see his under-utilised undercarriage when he looked down. In his head he was still in his prime.

Life continued to deal him shitty hand after shitty hand. He thought about the Cook girl. She was about nineteen or twenty. The girl he chatted up might have known her. He thought about Carrie and all that led to her drastic solution to the problems she'd become ensnared by. He thought about his Dad, minding his own business, dodging away, then a part of him breaks and it happens to be a part that's too vital to live without. He thought about his poor wee Mammy and all her struggles, all her stoicism, and her reward was to develop a cancer so bellicose, so ravenous, that it consumed her in the space of a year.

He drank more whisky and wallowed in self-pity, not watching the procession of pish that danced (sometimes literally) across the television in the corner of his mother's sitting room. He needed to break this cycle, get on with something more than the job and drinking by himself.

Not tonight, though.

Not tonight.

***

Texts and calls had been coming in all day and night from shocked and concerned friends. Colin ignored almost all of them, managing a couple of cursory replies before finding the whole process too draining. He lay on his bed, looking at the ceiling, lost inside his own thoughts.

The phone vibrated again and he glanced at the caller ID. Something had to be wrong with his eyes. He sat up and snatched the phone from the bedside table, swiping across the screen to bring it to life. His heart slowed, blood hammered in his temples, his stomach lurched. What the fuck was this? Some kind of sick joke? He began to tremble as he opened the message.

Hi, Coco. Do you miss me?

The message was from Debbie.

His vision contracted to a pin-prick before he was consumed by a nauseating, swirling blackness.

8.

When Stark opened the door, Duncan Cook was pacing up and down in the interview room, Colin and Grant Cook sitting on the plastic chairs provided. Colin fidgeting, biting his nails; Grant cross-armed and stone-faced. They both got to their feet as he came in.

"Hi, guys, thanks for coming in." Stark shook hands with all three of them in turn, gestured for them to sit and took his place opposite them.

"I've met Grant already but, just for the record, I'm Detective Inspector Adam Stark."

The two new Cooks nodded and mumbled in assent.

"Now, if I've got this right, Colin, you've received a text sent from Debbie's mobile phone – is that right?"

"Aye."

"Listen, mate, I don't know what kind of sick bastard is at work here but you better start getting your finger out an' catch them. You know what this means, don't you, eh? It means she didn't kill herself, that's what it means," interjected Duncan. He was red in the face, overwrought, one step away from foaming at the mouth. Unlike his brother, he appeared to have allowed comfortable living to soften him. He was a good two or three inches taller than his sibling but much heavier, with a significant midriff threatening to pop the buttons off the shirt he was wearing, a jowly face and, again in contrast to his brother, shaven-headed.

"Ok, Mr Cook, I understand emotions are running high here, but just let me get some facts down on paper first. Alright?"

"Dunc, just let the guy do his job," said Grant. "The sooner we get this done, the sooner he can get on wi' finding out what's going on, eh."

Stress flared out of every gesture and word from Duncan like the flames from the chimneys at Grangemouth refinery. Stark worried about the guy's health. The broken veins in his yellowish corneas, the gleam of sweat on his bald pate, and the nicotine-stained fingers suggested a man who could do without loading any further strain onto his circulatory system.

"Thanks, Grant. Now, Colin, tell me exactly how and when this all happened. Take your time and don't leave anything out. Small details can sometimes turn out to be important."

The boy retold his story. As he did so, Stark found himself in agreement with the boy's agitated father. This strongly suggested Debbie Cook's death was not as straightforward as they'd first thought.

"Did you reply to the text, Colin?" asked Stark.

"Naw, I was too shocked an' scared. Anyway, after I showed it to my dad, he told me we needed to let you lot know an' that I shouldn't reply to whoever this is." Colin's hands trembled as he spoke and his eyes glistened under the fluorescent lights of the interview room.

"Have you got the phone there with you, Colin?"

"Yeah," he said, handing it across to Stark.

"So, is Coco a nickname then?"

"Aye, it is. I don't really like it but I never minded Debbie calling me it as much as other folk."

"Right. I'd like to get our tech guys onto this. Is it ok if I keep the phone for the rest of today? I'll get it back to you as soon as we're finished analysing it."

"What? You'll have it all day?"

"Fuck's sake, Colin," roared Duncan, grabbing Colin by the front of his hooded sweatshirt, "your cousin's been murdered an' all you're worried about is your fuckin' phone!"

Stark put his hand on Duncan Cook's to persuade him to release his son. "Mr Cook, please calm down. This won't help anyone. I'm sure Colin will be happy to let us have the phone, won't you?"

The boy nodded, a tear leaking from the corner of his eye that he wiped away in the manner of someone hoping no-one else had noticed.

"So, what do you think this all means, DI Stark?" asked Grant Cook, who'd sat through his brother's outburst without reacting.

Stark sat back in his seat and skim read back across the notes he'd taken. "Well, I don't want to jump to conclusions. For instance, it might be possible that message is a rogue that was sent a while ago an' has just turned up by accident."

"Is that possible?"

"Aye, happens wi' me a fair bit. We just need to rule that out; that's one of the reasons I want the tech guys to look at it."

"Right, but what if it wasn't a rogue or an accident?" pressed Duncan Cook. His skin was almost puce now and his breathing sounded laboured. "What then?"

"Well, I have to say, it looks like somebody may have acquired Debbie's phone. If they have, we'll need to try and track them down and see how they came by it. Using Colin's nickname suggests it's someone that knows him well, and I know this sounds pretty sick, but it might be a prank. Somebody thinking they're being funny when they clearly aren't anything of the sort," said Stark.

"It better not be one of your dickhead mates pissing about, Colin. This isn't funny. Debbie's dead an' we need to find out why!" Duncan Cook looked on the verge of tears, his anger and frustration approaching boiling point.

"I don't think any of my friends would do that. That's beyond fucked up. They all know how close me and Debbie were. It can't be that. It can't be," said Colin, trying to maintain his cool in the face of his father's increasing hostility.

"Look, guys, I think it's important not to get too far

ahead of ourselves. We need to rule out the simple technological reasons first an' move on from there. Is there anything else you want to tell me about? Did you notice anything unusual about Debbie's behaviour in the days before she died?" Stark asked, directing his question more towards Colin than Duncan Cook.

The boy shook his head.

"Tell him about that idiot that tried to run you over the other night," snapped Duncan.

Stark tried to hide his surprise. "What? Someone tried to run you over, Colin?"

"I don't know if they did it on purpose, like, but it was all a bit weird. I was running, an' this car came up behind me, an' nearly knocked me down. I managed to dodge it but I buggered up my ankle an' couldn't walk. Next thing the driver stops, comes back to see what happened, but just stands there. Didn't help, didn't say anything, then just walked off and left me to it. Pissing wi' rain, freezing, an' no mobile to call for help."

"Right, that sounds a bit odd, did you know this guy?"

"I couldn't see very well coz my glasses came off but, no, I don't think so. Lucky my faither came out to look for me or it could have been a lot worse."

"Aye, what kind of arsehole does something like that, eh? He could have died of fuckin hypothermia!" said Duncan.

Stark could detect the genuine fatherly concern cloaked in the macho aggression.

"Did you get a look at the car?" continued Stark, trying not to let the high emotion derail his train of thought.

"Naw, it was dark, an' I'm blind as a bat without my specs. All I could see was some tail-lights I can't be sure what kind of motor it was."

"Alright, that's enough to be getting on wi' for now. I'll be briefing the team an' we'll get the tech guys on the case wi' the phone. As soon as we know anything, I'll be in touch, ok?"

They all stood and shook hands again.

"Thanks, son. I know you're doing your best. We just want to know why it happened, that's all," said Grant, his grip somehow even firmer than before.

"No bother," said Stark.

The phone on the table vibrated and the screen lit up. All four men froze. Stark broke the spell and picked it up.

Aw Coco, you in the huff wi me?

"What is it? Is that another message from that sick bastard?" spat Duncan Cook.

It took a moment for Stark's brain to re-engage with forming speech. "Ok, this changes everything. It's another message from Debbie's phone."

An uproar of outrage and expletives poured from the Cooks and it took Stark a moment or two to restore order.

"Colin, I need you to think about all your friends and how any of them might have gotten access to Debbie's phone. You need to think about who likes to wind you up by calling you Coco. I'll need a list of possible names as soon as you can get me them.

"Remember, sending these texts doesn't necessarily mean this person had anything to do wi' Debbie's death. You all need to try an' stay calm, stay focused on helping me an' my team. Once you've done your list, Colin, hand it in at the desk an' then get away home. We're not going to get to the bottom of this in the next few hours but we will get you some answers, eventually – that I can promise."

Another melee erupted but as it subsided and they began to accept his reassurances, Stark escorted all three men to the front desk. He needed to gather the troops and update the boss. He was getting less certain by the minute that the Cook girl killed herself after all.

Stark took some time updating McLaren and agreeing a plan of attack with him, before organising the team meeting.

Something was changing in his relationship with

McLaren. He could sense a grudging respect now, an understanding that Stark wasn't trying to be the big shot or get one over on his superior. It was also true that McLaren had been able to take a lot of credit for the relatively successful resolution of the McDuff situation. No dead children to bury always cheered up the top brass. If nothing else, McLaren was a pragmatist and if Stark could make him look better, the DCI would allow him to. Despite their rocky start and McLaren's apparent distrust, things were getting better. Working with McLaren was already ten times better than the nightmare he'd endured with his old boss in London, Morris Hargreaves. Stark didn't find himself being ranted at or denigrated during every encounter. Sure, there were still a few snide comments and an occasional put down, but their frequency was reducing all the time.

Once the team had been updated and a few tasks divided up, Stark took Barr aside.

"Ian, have you found anything in Debbie Cook's laptop yet?" asked Stark.

Barr looked a bit sheepish. "Sorry, sir. I've no' had time to look through it yet."

"What? Christ, Ian. Ok, give it to me. You can start interviewing her friends; see if any of them can shed some light on her frame of mind, worries, that sort of thing. We'll get the tech team to scan the computer for anything unusual."

It wasn't a regular occurrence but Barr was left in no doubt about Stark's annoyance.

"Yes, sir. Sorry, sir."

"I also want you to get the list of names Colin Cook's supposed to have left us. I think Rosemary should have it at the desk. Get one of the other DCs and a couple of uniforms to help you set up some interviews, ok?"

"Aye, no' bother, sir."

"We need to try an' find out who could've got a hold of

the lassie's phone an' why they're taunting Colin Cook with it. We need to get to the bottom of her last known movements, who was last to see her. The car thing is still bothering me, as well."

"I had a look, sir. She could get a bus to the services on the south side of the bridge an' walk from there. It's about a mile maybe."

Stark had to concede this provided a nice dose of initiative to balance out the computer slackness.

"That just doesn't seem right to me. The more I think about this, the more I think someone else drove her. They might only have dropped her off. Maybe they had a fight an' whoever it was drove away an' left her there, never thinking for a moment she'd do anything like jump ... or what's looking more an' more likely is she was taken there an' killed by someone who kept her phone to taunt Colin Cook with."

"How about that birdwatcher guy, Gilbert? The one that found her. Should we go have another word wi' him, sir?" asked Barr.

"Naw, I don't see the point. I mean, how would he know Cook's nickname?"

Barr looked crestfallen. "Aye, right enough."

Stark dropped into silence, thoughts flashing back and forth. "Actually, it's not totally out of the question, is it?"

"How d'you mean, sir?"

"Well, there could be older texts on the phone with Cook's nickname on them. I still don't think Gilbert's our man but now you've put the thought in my head, we'll need to rule him out. Put him on your list of folk to interview."

"Ok, sir. No worries."

Barr's self-esteem recovered enough for him to chance a wee grin.

9.

Colin Cook chinked glasses with Paul Jacobs.

"To Debbie."

"To Debbie," chimed Jacobs.

Both men took a healthy chug from their pints and then dropped into silence for a moment.

Debbie: more sister than cousin; a sweet, caring, funny girl; someone Colin could turn to when he needed help or advice – gone. His aunt and uncle were broken, his own parents almost as bereft. None of them could come to terms with the police assertion that she'd killed herself. It just couldn't be true. Colin replayed the last time he'd spoken to her in his head.

"Hey Coco," she'd chirped on the other end of the phone. She was the only one he genuinely liked using the lifelong nickname he hated – the clown connotations and potential for piss-taking were too high to ever be totally comfortable with it. But, when Debbie said it, it felt right; eternally childlike, innocent and affectionate. "You around at the weekend, hun?"

"I think so, why?"

"Fancy a wee blow-out up in Stirling on Saturday? A few of the Uni crowd are going out an' I thought you might like to come along. What do you think?"

"Aye, should be fine, Debs. Text me when you know what you're doing, eh."

"Great, brilliant. Should be a good night, Coco. Oh, and Alison will be there..." She gave him that playful giggle that was such a part of her.

He laughed, knowing she was only teasing. Colin had a massive crush on her friend Alison but, so far, he'd not built up the courage to do anything about it. "Ok, ok. I

61

know what you're getting at, Debs. We'll see, alright?"

"Yay! Got to go Coco, see you at the weekend. Love you, honey."

"Me too." His reply was always the same; reserve over reality. Regret swept over him at how he'd not been able to return her affection and love more openly.

The conversation took place the day before she died. Making plans, bright and breezy. Why would this person kill herself? Why? A dark thought crept up on him but he swatted it away. It couldn't be that. Not after all this time.

"I still can't take this in, Paul. Why? Why would she have done it?"

Jacobs shook his head and shrugged. "I have no idea, Coco. I have not got a fuckin' scooby."

Colin tolerated Paul calling him Coco as he'd done it since childhood and couldn't break the habit. It lacked Debbie's warmth and affection but it wasn't worth pulling him up for it. He never encouraged strangers or new acquaintances to follow suit.

"I keep thinking about what I should have done. How I should have known. Why didn't I know she was feeling so bad about something?" said Colin, his voice wavering, his emotions only just staying in check.

Paul Jacobs had few friends in the world; even fewer he could rely on when things went tits-up. Colin was the only one with whom he would reciprocate. Debbie was always a flake, a drama queen; she craved attention, validation, reassurance, and Colin always obliged. He was too soft, spent far too much time being her confidante and shoulder. It wasn't healthy. Debbie was his cousin, not his bloody girlfriend, and Paul had told Colin this straight before. But, even an insensitive, egotistical arse like Paul Jacobs knew there was a time and a place for hard truths, and standing in the pub just after she'd died wasn't it.

"Look, Coco, don't start blaming yourself, eh. Nobody saw this coming. It's not going to do any good thinking like that, man, ok?"

"Aye, but there's something really weird going on an' all. Somebody started sending me texts using her phone," said Colin quietly, voice quivering.

"What? Someone's texting you with Debbie's phone? You're sure about that?"

Colin nodded.

"Oh, fuck. That's not good. Have you been to the polis?"

"Aye. They're looking into it. What if she didn't kill herself, Paul? The polis reckon she chucked herself off the Clacks Bridge," Colin began to shake his head, "but I can't help thinking; what if someone took her there an' killed her? An' then I think, why would somebody do that? Why?" As tears began to fall, Jacobs put his arms around his friend and let him cry for a moment or two, before becoming aware of the quizzical looks they were getting from other patrons.

"Right, big man, let's go. You're no' fit for the pub. I'll take you home," said Paul, letting go of Colin and fishing for his car keys.

"Ok," was all Colin could manage.

Jacobs looked in his rear-view mirror and noticed the same 4x4 behind him as he'd seen earlier that day. The bull-bars on the front were what made it distinctive. Probably nothing. Alloa was a small place, chances were this was just a coincidence. He pulled into the supermarket car park and grabbed the shopping list. He liked to go shopping late at night. It meant he avoided the annoying bastards who pawed at him for autographs and, worst of all, wanted to take selfies with him. It also meant he encountered far fewer of the abusive morons as well.

He took out the phone and thought about sending a text. No, he'd leave it for now.

With the shopping done, he returned to his car. The groceries went in the passenger footwell, which was the only real space he had for such things in this car, and he took the trolley back to the designated area. Well, he took it *towards* the designated area. He couldn't be bothered walking all the way and just abandoned the trolley in the middle of some unoccupied parking bays. As far as he was concerned, the lad who was paid to take them back to the front of store could retrieve it; that's what he was there for after all. Jacobs was actually helping to maintain a justification for his position. This, in fact, made it an altruistic act.

Back at the car Jacobs opened the driver's door and was about to get in, when his attention was drawn to the 4x4. A jet black Range Rover, and fairly new by the look of it. He couldn't make out if anyone was sitting in the front seat due to the glare from the overhead light it was parked underneath. Closing the door again, Jacobs began to walk toward the car. As he did so, he heard the engine starting up before being dazzled by the full-beam of the headlights. Shielding his eyes from the blinding light, he realised the car was coming straight towards him. He dived sideways, tripping as he did so and crashed into a trolley somebody else had abandoned in a similar fashion to him. He yelled in pain as his hands, knees and head took the full brunt of the impact with both trolley and tarmac. The Range Rover roared past and off out of the car park.

Jacobs got up and tried to give chase but, by the time he'd disentangled himself from the trolley and checked all his limbs were intact, the driver had made good their escape. He walked back to his car, raging, sore and indignant. Getting into the car, he felt an odd sensation on his forehead. He pulled down the sun-visor and checked himself in the mirror on the back of it – a trickle of blood was sliding towards his left eye. He looked about for something to stem the flow with. No tissue paper, no handkerchief. As the blood reached his eyebrow and then dripped onto his cheek, he got out of the car and wiped it with his hand. It was not long before more arrived. He walked back down to the store to get something to staunch the blood with and to get cleaned up.

The security guard at the entrance to the store reacted with wide-eyed surprise at the bloodied figure heading for the toilets.

"Excuse me, sir? Are you ok?" he said as he made to follow Jacobs.

Jacobs turned to answer without breaking stride. "Aye, I'm fine. I tripped, split my head. No big deal. I'll sort it out."

The guard stopped and let him go. It wasn't his job to act as a nurse or a doctor and, if the guy was going to be so rude about it, why should he help?

Jacobs cleaned himself up, pressed a paper towel against the wound, then went out into the shop and bought a packet of sticking plasters. With repairs completed, he went back to the car. Starting up the engine, his mobile pinged to signify the receipt of a text message. He ignored it and drove out of the car park.

***

Stark scrolled through the options he'd been sent as part of his free-trial. It wasn't going to be easy deciding which one to go with. He hadn't paid any money out, yet, so the info they sent him was limited and didn't have photos. This made choosing anyone all the harder. How much of the stuff in these profiles was embellishment, half-truth or outright lies? Delusion and self-deception would be rife among these women, he was sure of it. Of course, he'd tell anyone who asked that he'd filled in his own form with scrupulous honesty but, as a policeman, he was only too aware of the lengths some people would go to when they were desperate. And that's how he felt – desperate. It wasn't an emotion he enjoyed. He slurped down some whisky and topped up the glass again. He didn't think he could do this. It wasn't him.

I'm nineteen. Those words, the humiliation, nagged at

65

him again. Was *that* him? Trying to pull teenagers in a bar. Was that a better alternative?

There was one profile he kept coming back to. Professional woman, no kids, never married. That would reduce complications considerably. The only issue would be looks. Shallow? Maybe, but he wasn't an unquestioning subscriber to the inner beauty thing. He didn't expect an underwear model but he wouldn't be happy with a hammer thrower. He was allowed one email and if she replied, he'd have to join up proper and pay his dues. There was no harm in giving it a go. However, embarrassment alone was not stopping him. The real problem lay in being a policeman; trained to analyse and weigh up options, naturally suspicious, prone to look out for a dark side, an ulterior motive. He closed the computer without following through with the contact and went to sit on the couch.

The Cook girl drifted into his thoughts. He turned the information they'd accumulated so far over in his head, trying to decide whether the texts really did indicate murder or just some kind of sick mind game. He felt his guilt about Carrie swell inside his chest. A blackness approached that he'd come to recognise. He sank another whisky and topped up the glass, trying to numb the worst of the pain.

***

Cammy McDuff parked up and stepped out of the car. All that illegal, under-age driving had stood him in good stead when it came to passing his test early. Two days after his seventeenth birthday, he sailed through the test with only one small advisory.

He sparked up a cigarette and exhaled into the dark. With summer on the way, and daylight hours stretching out, he'd expected it to be a bit less nippy. Then again, it was Scotland; he really shouldn't have been so naive. He took out his mobile phone and scrolled through the photos, re-checking everything and reassuring himself. Stubbing out the cigarette, he went into the house.

After the dust of his brother's kidnapping and his dad's jailing had settled, Cammy's mum bought him a two bedroom house in Stirling from her lottery winnings. She wanted to separate him from some of his unsavoury friends, whom she believed would be lining up to bleed him dry if he stayed in the scheme in Alloa. He'd tried to get her to buy something in Alloa, but it was Stirling or nothing, and Stirling was by far the better option. He'd never seen eye-to-eye with Stella. She favoured his older brother, and never made any secret of the fact. Despite her generosity in giving him the house and a monthly allowance no job he was qualified for could ever provide him with, he wasn't grateful. He resented being second best, overlooked, criticised incessantly and, even though he wanted to be free of her, he found her relish for ejecting him from her household hurtful. He also missed being looked after.

The place was a tip. He'd never cooked anything more challenging than beans on toast; and even that most basic of culinary delights rarely graced his table. The washing-up was done on an emergency basis only; a sort of one-in-one-out system, which meant a permanent scattering of crockery and utensils throughout the house. The ashtrays looked like spoil heaps from an open-cast coal mine. He owned a vacuum cleaner but it wasn't going to suffer from wear and tear. Bottles, cans, takeaway cartons, and magazines took the place of ornaments. Cases for computer games lay here and there, the correct disc rarely returned to them once he'd finished playing. He was always running out of basics like bread and milk and in any case, his fridge constituted a major health hazard – if he could have squeezed food into the gaps between the alcohol. His mum had tried to tidy up a couple of times but gave up when she realised the scale of the task and the likelihood that he'd set about restoring the shambles almost as soon as she'd left his driveway. The only thing she did for him now was his washing, which he took round to hers when he ran out of vital items of clothing.

Most days Cammy returned to this midden and vowed to change his ways. Most days he was kidding himself on.

He went through to the kitchen and took a bottle of beer from the fridge, twisted off the cap, letting it drop onto the worktop next to its cohorts and went back through to the living room. He sat down on his couch, grabbed the controller, fired up the TV and games console and set about destroying the inhabitants of a distant galaxy. The doorbell chimed just as he was about to complete his level and hyper warp onto a new planet. The distraction caused him to disintegrate in a stream of alien laser fire and he wasn't too happy about it. He flung the controller onto the floor and stomped to the door.

Badger grinned and held up a carrier bag full of cans. "Bevvy?" he asked as he pushed past Cammy and headed for the couch.

"Aye, come in why don't you?" said Cammy.

As Cammy walked back into the living room, Badger held out a can, which Cammy took despite still having an almost full bottle on the go. "Cheers."

"How's tricks, Cammy?" asked Badger, the breezy tone indicating alcohol might not have been his only drug of choice that evening.

Cammy slumped onto the couch along from Badger. "Aye, fine. How?"

"I think I've got some good news for you, my man."

Cammy looked at the ceiling. Usually, such pronouncements from Badger meant something to do with cheap drugs or a car he'd identified as ripe for ringing. All fine and good but not worth interrupting his game for at half eleven at night.

"No, really, you'll like this, eh," added Badger, spotting his friend's irritation.

"Really? How very fuckin mysterious. What is it?"

"Let's just say I've found someone to help make sure we don't get caught teaching that prick Paul Jacobs his lesson."

Cammy smiled. "Aye? Tell me more."

10.

Ian Barr knocked on Graham Gilbert's door and stood back a step or two. The place was unremarkable; a mid-terrace house with a small, scruffy, front garden, which amounted to little more than two patches of mossy lawn bisected by a path of concrete slabs. The only separation from neighbours and the street was a single slat of low-level wooden fencing.

Gilbert answered the door in a state of half-undress. Barr was grateful he'd chosen to cover the bottom half.

"Can I help you?" asked Gilbert.

"Mr Gilbert, I'm Detective Constable Barr and this is PC McKay. You may remember we spoke to you down at Kennetpans when you found the girl in the river?"

"Oh, aye, right. What do you want from me, now? I went down the station an' gave my statement like I said I would, eh."

"Yes, Mr Gilbert, I know that. We just want to ask you a few more questions. Can we come in, please?"

Gilbert looked up and down the street and glanced back into his house. "Well, the place is a bit, you know. I wasn't really expecting visitors. I was still in bed, eh."

Barr glanced at his watch, by instinct rather than necessity.

"I work shifts," said Gilbert flatly.

"Right, well, that's ok, we'll only take a few minutes of your time," replied Barr.

"Alright, come in, then," said Gilbert holding open the door and pointing to his left. "Go into the front room, I'm just going to get a t-shirt."

Barr and McKay went into the room indicated and sat down on the couch. The room was small, untidy but clean enough, and looked as if it was a couple of decades since it was last decorated. The smell of stale tobacco hung in the air and nicotine had yellowed the wallpaper. After a minute or so, Gilbert returned. His t-shirt was from a Genesis tour in 1986. A bit like his front room, it was faded and ill-fitting.

"So, what is it you need to ask me, then?" mumbled Gilbert as he lit a roll-up and sat down in the armchair. It presumably once matched the couch but was now a pale shadow of its former self thanks to its exposure to direct sunlight through the bay window.

"We just want to go through your statement again, make sure we haven't missed anything important, eh," said Barr. "One thing I forgot to ask you that morning was whether or not you'd noticed a mobile phone anywhere near the girl?"

"No, she was in the water an' I never touched her, so how would I have?"

"Ok, just checking, sir. Did you know Debbie Cook, or any of her family?"

"No' really. I've seen their lorries about the place but I don't know them personally, like."

Barr scribbled notes, watching Gilbert's body language. There was something about this guy he didn't like; nothing specific, just a feeling, a sense that he was hiding something. He'd felt it at the scene when they first met. "I wonder if I could use your toilet, Mr Gilbert?"

"Erm, aye, ok. Top of the stairs, door straight in front of you."

Barr climbed the stairs to the landing. There were three plain, white, wooden doors. The bathroom straight ahead and the two others he presumed were bedrooms. All three were ajar. He pushed open the door of the room closest to the bathroom and looked in. It was darkened by a blackout blind across the window so he flicked on the light switch.

The furniture comprised a chair and a large desk sporting an iMac, complete with what looked like a state-of-the-art printer. Piles of paper were stacked on and around the desk. The walls were adorned with a myriad of photographs. Some were of landscapes or sunsets but the majority were of birds. Barr was no expert but they looked decent quality. As he scanned across, he felt his heart jump from his chest to his throat. One wall was dedicated to the Cook girl's death. Newspaper clippings and photos. Photos from the scene. Photos Gilbert must have taken himself. Alarm bells began to ring in Barr's head. However, he was up here under the pretence of going to the loo and he had no warrant or probable cause to justify a search. The last thing he wanted was to screw this up on a technicality. He took a couple of quick snaps with his phone camera and switched off the light. He stepped into the bathroom and flushed the toilet, before returning downstairs.

Barr reclaimed his seat next to McKay. "As a matter of interest, Mr Gilbert, do you ever take photos of the birds you go to see?"

Gilbert shrugged, "No' really. I prefer to sketch anything rare that I find. I'm old school, don't like to rely on technology, eh. How? What's that got to do with what happened to that lassie?"

"Oh, nothing, I'm just getting as much background info as possible. You'd be amazed at how things end up being connected that don't seem important to begin with, eh."

Barr watched Gilbert shuffle in his seat and look away out the window. The lie about the photography worried him. It had been instant, coolly done. Too coolly. Barr needed to get out of here and get back with a warrant as soon as he could.

"Ok, Mr Gilbert, that'll do us for now. Thanks for your co-operation. If we need you for anything else I'll get back in touch."

"Did you get anything useful from the Cook laddie's

phone, Calum?" asked Stark.

Calum Murphy worked in the tech section and was generally regarded as a good guy and a good technician. A bit geeky, sure, but not one of those types who deals with the less technologically inclined with infuriating smugness or irksome condescension.

"Not an awfy lot, Adam. The texts were sent at the time they said they were, which rules out some kind of glitch or delay. No way to tell an exact location where they were sent from though, as they didn't have any GPS or location services switched on. The best I could do is give you the tower the signals were relayed by."

"Ok, that's a shame but at least we know it was sent in real time. That's one clarification we needed. Email me the tower locations an' I'll have a look anyway. Have any more texts turned up from Debbie Cook's phone?"

"Not since I've had it, no."

"Are you finished wi' it?"

"Yep."

"Right, good. I'll come round an' pick it up just now. I'm off to see the owner an' I promised I would return it once you were done wi' it," said Stark. "By the way, I'm bringing round Debbie Cook's laptop for you to have a look at. I've been through the emails and documents in obvious places and found nothing of any note. Can you give it the once over for anything hidden or covertly stored?"

"No bother, Adam, I'll have a look. See you in a bit. Cheers."

"Good stuff. Thanks, Calum."

Ian Barr walked back into the office as Stark put the phone down. "Ian, how are you getting on wi' that list of names from Colin Cook?"

"I was going to start on the interviews today, sir. Thing is, I think you need to see this first, eh," said Barr, holding out his mobile phone.

Stark took it from him and looked at the photo.

"Where the hell did you get this?"

"That guy Gilbert, sir. Something about him was bothering me, so I pretended to use his bog and had a wee nosy about upstairs. This was taking up a whole wall in his back room."

"Jesus, we forgot to ask him about a camera or photies when we saw him at the scene. I should have known a birdwatcher would be into photography. Bloody schoolboy error.

"Did he give you permission to look about, Ian?"

"No' exactly, sir. I didn't let on that I'd taken this or seen the wall. I was worried about legal technicalities an' all that, eh."

"Good. We need a pretext for going back to search, now. We all know the kind of person who has a trophy wall an' takes souvenirs from crime scenes. We need to get this dodgy bastard in here as soon as. Nice work, Ian, looks like your instinct was spot on," said Stark, patting Barr heftily on the shoulder.

"Cheers, boss," replied a red-faced Barr.

Graham Gilbert looked rattled. He persistently fidgeted with his greasy hair and scruffy beard, avoiding eye-contact when answering the questions Stark put to him.

"Come on, Graham, I need to know. Why did you take photos of a dead girl? Were they keepsakes? Trophies? Reminders of what a great job you'd done?"

"I didn't kill her, I swear. I just found her, eh. I don't know why I took the photos. It was stupid, crazy," replied Gilbert, his voice trailing off.

"Crazy. An interesting choice of word, Graham. Is that going to be your defence is it? Insanity? Diminished responsibility? Did voices inside your head tell you to kill that innocent young girl?"

"I didn't fucking kill her, ok!" shouted Gilbert, wild eyes darting to meet Stark's for the first time, desperate to be believed. "I just have a thing for serial killers an' all that stuff. I shouldn't have done it but I couldn't help it. I thought maybe I could help wi' the investigation; find out something you missed." He slumped in his chair and a tear rolled down his cheek.

"Well, that was very big of you, Graham, but watching a couple of episodes of Sherlock doesn't qualify you to become a detective. I'm going to leave this for now. We'll start again in a bit, once you've had time to think about telling me what really happened."

Stark suspended the interview and made his way back to his office while Gilbert returned to a cell. DCI McLaren, who'd been observing, was waiting for him, sipping from a mug of tea.

"You think he did it?"

"No' sure, sir. He's a bit odd, a bit non-standard but I don't get that vibe off him of killer, you know? There's no arrogance, no superiority. He's not calm or composed at all."

"Yeah, I'm wi' you on that, Stark. He's a strange one alright but I'm no' convinced he's a murderer either."

"We'll keep plugging away an' see if he cracks. He might be a great actor or this was some kind of tragic accident. Whatever the case, it's no' right that he took photos of the girl and stuck them up on his wall."

"No, it certainly is not," said McLaren.

**

Colin felt the need to go for a run become overwhelming. His body was habituated to the rush of endorphins it produced and his long, lean frame wasn't well suited to sitting about, folded up on itself for long periods. The ankle wasn't as badly injured as he'd first feared and he decided it was time to test it out. He hadn't been on the road since the incident with the silent stranger and, as he set off, he felt a flutter of nerves in his gut.

The night air was mild, the breeze minimal, the clouds

too thin to threaten dampening his return to the road. This time he had invested in an armband where he could put his mobile phone. The vulnerability and uncertainty of being stranded at the roadside was something he wouldn't be repeating. It also meant he could listen to music as he ran. He never bothered with an accompanying beat before, preferring to take in the sounds of the night around him. However, with the option easily available to him, he dialled up his *Kings of Leon* playlist and picked up the pace.

He ran as if his shoes were a pair of mini hovercraft. A strange, unexpected turn of events. He was sure that after more than a week away, his body would have become soft, uncooperative, petulant even – particularly his unpredictable ankle. As the pumping chorus of *Sex On Fire* filled his head, he let his mind drift away from sadness and worry. Not so much him running along the road as the road flowing away under him like a river.

The traffic was mercifully light; only one car passed him, and with plenty of respect for his personal space. His pace rose without him consciously deciding it should. The music set the tempo and he wondered why he'd never done this before. Exercise and entertainment; food for body and soul.

When the text alert cut through the music with obnoxious alacrity, he started, stumbled in an unseen pothole and sprawled. All that good work undone in an instant. He felt pain sear through his ankle at the same time as hands and knees scraped across the tarmac. He managed to avoid a face-plant and, this time, his glasses stayed put thanks to the elastic headband he'd bought at the same time as the armband.

Colin stood up. Both hands and knees were grazed but only his left knee seemed to be bleeding. His ankle was very sore but, all things considered, it could have been a lot worse. Unlike the last time, he could at least put enough weight on it to limp. One thing was certain; he wouldn't be running any further tonight.

He took the phone from its holster, switched off the music and removed his headphones. He opened up the text message and felt his vision swim, his heart race, heat sweep over him.

Oh Coco, it's time to stop running. Don't you think?

Colin stared at the message. Fury thundered through him and he dialled the number, hands shaking, emotions cartwheeling. It rang a couple of times and then went to voicemail. As he listened to Debbie sing-song her encouragement to leave a message, the storm cloud of rage evaporated. Grief shuddered through him and he sat down on the kerb, the phone no longer pressed against his ear. He was vaguely aware of a car passing as he sat there but he couldn't have cared any less about the rest of the world at that moment.

11.

Stark called the team together for a meeting. The latest text sent to Colin Cook was top of the agenda. The Cooks arrived mob-handed that morning as soon as he started his shift, blazing with indignity and fear. They demanded action and both Stark and DCI McLaren promised they'd apply the full gamut of resources available to them in an attempt to resolve things.

"This new text has changed the complexion of the case again. I think we can safely say Graham Gilbert isn't sending those texts. If he's no' the one doing that, I think it's less likely he killed Debbie Cook. Of course, he might not have been alone but, given his personality an' lifestyle, that seems unlikely as well. We'll keep him in custody for now, keep questioning him, but we need to find this person who's texting, and soon," said Stark. "The family are very anxious and, with the funeral coming up, they want this sorted out. I really want this sorted out too."

"Did we get any info from the Cook lad's phone, sir?" asked one of the constables.

"Nothing much. It might help eventually but, for now, it's not locking us into any one spot. We do know the texts are being sent from locations around Central region. Not that surprising, I suppose, but at least we won't have to look too far afield for whoever is doing this. I still think a friend or associate is the most likely culprit. Ian, how did you get on with interviewing the folk from Cook's list?"

Ian Barr took out his notepad and started flicking through it as he spoke. "I spoke to three guys so far but none of them seemed to harbour any obvious grudges or ill-will towards Cook. One of them claimed they hadn't seen him for a while and one claimed to be unaware that

Debbie Cook was dead. The last one lives in London, so I think we can rule him out right away. My gut feeling is that neither of the other two are a good fit for doing anything like this either.

"There is one interesting thing about this list though, sir."

"Uh-huh?"

"The footballer, Paul Jacobs, is on it."

Stark frowned. "A footballer called Jacobs? That rings a bell. Is he famous?"

Barr smiled. "No' really, sir. He plays in the lower leagues but his uncle is a famous ex-footballer – Jonny Jacobs."

"Right, of course! I mind of him having a nephew that played as well – now you've said it."

"Paul Jacobs is a bit of a tosser, though," said Barr. "Actually, the laddie's a grade-A tit!"

"How d'you mean?" asked Stark. "Do you know him personally, like?"

"Well, no, but I've read some of the stuff he's said in the papers, eh. An' the way he acts on the field; thinks he's bloody Lionel Messi or something. He plays in Scottish League Two, for Christ's sake!"

"Is he the guy who got himself into a bit of bother last week for giving the crowd the finger? I half read the back of a newspaper an' saw a picture but didn't connect the dots."

Barr laughed. "*Crowd* might be stretching it mind you, but aye, that's right, sir. In fact, I was there."

"Oh, right," said Stark.

"My faither's a life-long fan of East Fife an' they were playing Jacobs' mob that day. Pumped them 5-1, an' when that wee tit Jacobs gave the home fans the finger some gorilla took exception an' went after him. It was pretty funny, though, eh. The big eejit slipped and slid all over the place. Didn't manage to lay a hand on Jacobs before he got hauled away by the stewards an' then our lot came to get him."

"Doesn't sound like Jacobs is likely to win player of the season then."

"Naw, I wouldn't have thought so, sir. I read he had some kind of dressing-room row with his captain, Frank Dawson, after the game an' all; left the guy wi' a broken leg. Rumour is that Dawson's finished an' out the game for good because of it."

Stark leant back in his chair. "Christ, that's what you call adding injury to insult. I wonder how the Cook laddie knows him?"

"No' sure. Maybe they went to school together?" suggested Barr.

"Maybe. I'm going to see Colin Cook in a bit so I'll ask. Hold off interviewing Jacobs until after I've got some gen, ok?"

"No bother, sir."

Stark rubbed the back of his neck. "Ok, an' what about Debbie Cook's friends? How did we get on wi' them?"

"I only interviewed one lassie. An old school friend who'd lost touch wi' her since she went to Uni. She said they were never best pals but she was shocked to hear she'd killed herself, eh. The other interviews were done by PC Smith and DC Connelly. They said all her pals were devastated by her death and couldn't understand the suicide angle. Didn't see it coming; never had a clue that she was feeling that bad. One of them did say she thought she'd been a bit quieter than normal that week, but nothing to suggest she'd do something so drastic."

"What about last known movements?" asked Stark.

"A classmate from Uni, Alison Ogilvie, saw her get on a bus away from the campus on the afternoon of her death. She said Cook looked fine, said cheerio as normal. Nothing suspicious." replied Barr.

"Right, let's get going on some more actions. Ian, go an' get the laptop from Calum Murphy an' have another trawl through it. He says he's found nothing untoward; no hidden partitions in the hard drive, no encrypted files or folders. I've already had a look but another scan isn't going to do any harm." Stark was going to return it to her parents but decided to hang onto it for now. Although he'd not found anything that jumped out at him as useful evidence, he wasn't convinced they knew what they were looking for at the moment – especially until they tracked down who was doing the texting.

"Connelly, you an' Smith go down to Kennetpans an' do a door to door on those cottages near where she was found; see if anyone noticed Gilbert doing anything suspicious. The DCI has been in contact wi' the press. He's going to give them a briefing an' ask for help in finding out more about Debbie Cook's last knowns. However, I want this texting thing kept out of the public domain for now, otherwise it'll get sensationalised an' twisted by the media an' we'll be bombarded wi' spurious information. That's enough to be getting on wi' for now. Keep in touch, an' make sure I'm first to know if you turn anything up."

The room cleared and Stark returned to his office to gather his coat, keys and notepad.

Margo Cook put his tea down on the table in front of Stark and took a seat beside her son. Stark thought Colin Cook looked wrung out. Eyes like two piss-holes in the snow. Fidgeting and restless.

"Here's your phone, son." said Stark, handing it over.

"Ta. Did you find anything out from it?"

"Not much. The texts weren't delayed, so we know they weren't sent by Debbie, but we couldn't trace where they came from exactly without any GPS data."

"Right. Debbie always said that stuff was only on the phone for Big Brother to keep track of you. She always switched it off. I thought she was just being paranoid."

Colin took a deep breath in instalments. His mother put her hand on his leg.

"Sorry," he whispered, "it's been really hard to take, eh."

"It's alright, Colin. I understand. We'll take our time but it's important we try an' find out who could have taken Debbie's phone. I know I've asked you before, but do you have any idea what Debbie was up to in the days leading up to her death?"

"No, not really. She called me to arrange to go out the weekend after … after it happened. She seemed happy. I assumed she was just going to Uni as usual, out with her mates, that sort of thing, eh."

"And how about Paul Jacobs? You put his name on your list. How do you two know each other?"

"Been mates since we were little. Lived near each other an' went to the same schools."

"I assume he knew Debbie really well, then?" asked Stark, looking up from his notes.

"Aye, we were all very close growing up. Like brothers and sisters."

"And what about lately? Still as close?" asked Stark.

Colin looked away, eyes glistening, Adam's apple bobbing, breathing erratic.

"Detective Stark, I think this is getting too much for Colin. He's been through so much in the past few days. I think he needs a break."

It seemed to Stark that Margo Cook was making the request as much for her own sake as her son's.

"I appreciate that, Mrs Cook, but I only have a couple of more questions for now an' then I'll be on my way," said Stark. "So, I take it you an' Paul are not so close these days, Colin?"

"No' really, no. Football takes up a lot of his time. He's still my oldest mate, my best mate. He came over an' took me out for a beer the other night … after …"

"Aye, fair enough, son. You don't think it could be him sending the texts, then?"

Colin's eyes blazed. "No! There's no way Paul would

ever do anything like that. He loved Debbie, like I did, eh. I only put him on the list so you could rule him out straight away. He still calls me Coco but he's done it since we were wee kids. I don't mind him calling me it. It was him and Debbie."

His voice cracked and he battled to regain composure.

"Alright, son. That'll do for now. If we need to talk to you again, we'll give you a bell," said Stark. "Oh, an' if you get any more messages, let me know right away. Ok?"

Colin Cook nodded.

Stark stood and Margo Cook followed suit.

"It's fine, Mrs Cook, no need to get up, I'll see myself out," said Stark.

She nodded and sat back down, putting her arm around her son's shoulders.

Stark sat down at his desk and typed up his notes, printed them off and added them to the case file. He was pleased to see Barr had added the list of names from Colin Cook and he dialled the number for Paul Jacobs. It rang four or five times before going to answer machine. He left a message asking him to call back and hung up.

He noticed Rosemary from the front desk doing some photocopying and went over to say hello. She was a nice woman, always cheery, always helpful and very efficient.

"Hi, Rosemary. How are you doing?"

"Hi, Adam. Good thanks. How's things wi' you?"

"No' too bad. Been working on the Cook case. It's a bit of a difficult one, you know."

She pursed her lips and nodded. "It's dreadful. Lovely young lassie like that, dead too soon. I'll no' miss being so close to these sorts of cases, Adam. They really break my heart. I'm too soft, you ken what I mean?"

It took a moment for this to register with Stark but the light eventually went on. "Are you leaving, Rosemary? I didn't realise."

She gave him a wistful smile. "Aye. I thought everyone

knew. I'm taking the voluntary redundancy. Since the shake-up I've been swamped an' it's just got too much. I'm going to take a wee break an' then look to get something part-time, maybe, eh."

"Oh, right. That's a real shame. I'll really miss you."

She smiled and gently squeezed his hand. "Thanks, that's a nice thing to say. I'm no' going to miss the job but I'm going to miss the people."

"When are you going?"

"Next week. I'm having a wee leaving do on Friday. We're having a glass of fizz and some nibbles after work. It'd be nice if you could come along."

"Aye, of course. Thanks. I'll be there."

"Good," she said and walked back towards the reception area.

When he arrived at Jacobs' flat, Stark couldn't help thinking it wasn't the sort of place the footballer would like people to imagine he lived in. It wasn't a hovel by any means but it fell a long way short of the archetypal, swanky, luxury penthouse. Swanky. Stark thought it should have a silent *s* when applied to most professional footballers. Of course, Jacobs was only playing part-time football for now and that probably helped to explain the rather mundane lodgings. Stark frowned as he noticed the bright yellow Porsche parked outside. It could only belong to the footballer and, assuming it did, looked like a visible statement of his defiance, or even denial, of this underemployment.

It took Jacobs a few seconds more than seemed necessary to answer the bell. It felt deliberate to Stark; his hackles rose in anticipation of meeting the guy Barr described as a grade-A tit.

"Hello?"

"Mr Jacobs? It's Detective Inspector Adam Stark."

"Right. Come up."

The buzzer released the main door and Stark climbed

the three sets of stairs to Jacobs' front door, which he found ajar but with no host waiting to let him in. He closed the door behind him, muttering curses under his breath. He followed the hallway down to the living room and found Jacobs looking out of the window. He turned as Stark entered; offered no handshake or seat.

"So, Detective Stark, how can I help you?"

Insincere and brimming with his own self-importance. Barr had been right.

"As I said in my message, I'd like to talk to you about Debbie and Colin Cook. I understand you know or rather, in Debbie's case, knew them both well."

"Aye, we grew up together. Terrible thing about Debbie but there you go, eh."

Stark looked at Jacobs. Hands in pockets, smaller than he'd expected, head-to-toe in designer clobber – handsome, but he knew it. This rather offhand remark about Debbie surprised him.

"You don't seem too upset about it."

Jacobs shrugged. "Nothing I can do to change it. She decided life wasn't worth living, an' that killing herself was the answer. Selfish, attention-seeking behaviour if you ask me."

Stark frowned. "Really?"

"Och, aye. Look, we were close as kids, an' I still liked Debbie, but she was a drama queen. She loved to blow things out of proportion, get Coco running after her, which he always did. She was spoiled, used to getting what she wanted. Maybe someone said no for once an' she couldn't handle it? Who knows, eh."

Stark tried to read him, see if this was some kind of bluff disguising grief but he appeared to mean it. The lack of self-awareness and compassion was amazing.

"And what about Colin? How is he feeling about it?"

"He's devastated, of course. I take it you've talked to him? He loved her like a sister, even though she played him like a bloody fiddle, eh."

"Have you spoken to him about what happened?"

Jacobs walked across the room and sat in one of the armchairs. "Aye. We went out for a wee drink but he was too upset, so I took him home again."

"Has he mentioned anything about some texts he's been getting?" asked Stark, looking for a reaction as he took a seat of his own accord on the settee opposite Jacobs.

"Aye, he says somebody's been sending him texts using Debbie's phone. Seems a bit weird. Coco seems to think it means she was murdered an' this guy sending the texts killed her. I can't see it myself."

"Do you always call him Coco?"

Jacobs shrugged. "Probably. It's a habit. Been calling him that since primary school. Why?"

"The person sending the texts is calling him Coco. It suggests it's someone who knows him well."

A veil of anger crossed Jacobs' face. "And you think it might be me? Are you kidding me on?" His voice rose and he stood up from his seat and moved towards Stark. "This is a fuckin joke, right? Are you telling me you came round here to get me to confess to this bullshit?"

Stark also stood, making his height advantage clear to Jacobs and halting his advance. "Mr Jacobs, calm down. I never accused you of anything."

"Maybe not directly, but that's what you meant. Does Coc ... Colin know you're round here harassing me like this?"

"Harassing you? Mr Jacobs, one of your friends is dead in potentially suspicious circumstances and another is being terrorised by someone who has gotten hold of her mobile phone. I think you should be grateful we're taking this all so seriously and trying to rule out all possibilities, don't you? It was Colin gave us your name. He wants this person found as soon as possible and was willing to do anything to help – what about you, Mr Jacobs?"

The footballer thrust his hands back in his pockets and

walked over to the window. "Of course I want to help. I just resent being accused of something like that. I can't believe Coco sent you here to make sure it wasn't me." He shook his head and continued to look out of the window.

"As an aside: you play part-time football, right?"

Jacobs turned round, face darkening again, "And so what if I do, eh? I'll be moving on soon enough. I'm heading for the Premiership. This is just a stepping stone."

"Right. And that Porsche outside; is that yours?"

"Aye, it is, and what's that got to do wi' Debbie?"

"Nothing really, just surprised somebody who's only working part-time can afford such an expensive motor."

Jacobs began to advance again, then seemed to think better of it. His face flushed and his voice trembled. "Not that it's any of your business, but my dad bought me the car, alright?"

Stark decided to let him cool off. "Ok, fair enough, Mr Jacobs. He must be a generous man, your father. I'll leave you my card an' if you think of anything that might help us with our enquiries, please give me a call."

Jacobs watched Stark leave the room and returned to looking out the window. He lost track of time as his head swam with all the differing thoughts and emotions tumbling around in it. It was anger that kept coming to the fore. He couldn't say how long he'd been staring into the street before he noticed the Range Rover. The one with the bull bars. He tried to get eyes on the driver but his angle was wrong and the car a bit too far away. Jacobs raced down the stairs, taking them almost three and four at a time, burst out into the street and started running full tilt. About fifty metres from his quarry, they started the engine and pulled away with a squeal of tyres. In seconds they were out of sight. Jacobs ran back to his car, got in and drove after them. It was a waste of time; the scheme his flat was in provided a plethora of options for escape. They were long gone. Jacobs stopped the car and felt his adrenaline subside, replaced by fear. Who was this person, and why were they watching him?

12.

Stark left Gilbert in the interview room and went next door into the observation suite.

"Sir, I'm getting nowhere with this guy and, to be honest, I really don't think he killed her. His story is too consistent considering how nervous an' flustered he is. Usually, somebody like that would have slipped up by now, caught themselves out. We know he didn't send the texts and we've no' been able to find any previous links to the Cook girl."

"I think you're right, Stark. I've been waiting for him to catch himself out, tell a porky differently second time around, but it's just no' happened. What about forensics?" asked McLaren.

"They've turned up nothing either. His DNA isn't on the lassie and, so far, there's no traces of hers at his house or in his car but they've only just started on that job. I think we're going to have to let him go with a caution for taking the photos an' keep an eye on him."

McLaren shrugged and nodded, "The big bosses probably won't be too pleased but, aye, that looks about the size of it."

The party was in full swing when Stark walked into the canteen. It was a good turnout; not surprising given the length of Rosemary's service and the fact that she was well liked. Stark scanned the room. The DCI was there with his wife. DC Connelly, PC McKay, Jane and Wilma from reception with partners, a few more constables, a couple of the community support guys, a couple of techs, but no Ian Barr.

Stark saw Rosemary and walked towards her. She was

talking to a tall woman with her back to him. As he approached, Rosemary smiled and the tall woman looked over her shoulder. She was gorgeous and looked familiar but he couldn't think why. She smiled, making him a little wary. It's always awkward in a social setting when recognition is a one-way process.

"Adam, lovely to see you. So glad you could make it," said Rosemary, placing a hand on his shoulder and pecking him on the cheek. "This is my friend, Madeline. Madeline, this is Adam."

"Yes, we've met before," said the tall beauty and it all came back to Stark. She was the bank manager who tried to help Stella McDuff when her husband and brother-in-law attempted to take her lottery winnings from her. He held out his hand and, as she took it, the same spark of electricity that flew between them before completed a circuit of his nervous system.

"Ah, of course, *Ms* Short," he said, a mischievous grin spreading across his face, "nice to see you again. Assuming you are still *Ms*?"

She laughed and Rosemary looked puzzled. "Oh, it's a little joke, Rosie. We met during rather stressful circumstances and I chastised Adam for assuming I was *Mrs* Short. How are you, Adam?"

"I'm ok, thanks. How are you?"

"Yes, good, thanks."

An awkward silence began to develop and Rosemary cut in, "Right, I better mingle. Why don't you look after Madeline for me Adam while I do my hostess-with-the-mostest thing?"

Madeline blushed and Stark smiled in sympathy. Still, he was glad to be left alone with her. She was even more attractive than he remembered from that day in the bank. He also recalled Barr ribbing him about how he'd been lusting after her and his rather weak denials. They'd be even weaker now.

"Sorry about that," she said. "You don't really have to

look after me, you know."

"Oh, no, it's ok. Unless you'd rather I left you alone, of course?"

"Ha ha! No, it really is nice to see you again. I'm glad it's in more sociable surroundings this time, though." She pushed her long black hair behind her ear and took a sip of her wine. Stark realised he didn't have a drink and grabbed a glass of red from a nearby table.

"Cheers," he said clinking his glass against hers.

"Cheers," she replied and they both took a drink.

Stark winced at the harsh after-taste of the cheap plonk. "Ooft, that's erm, robust."

Madeline laughed, "I've got the white and it's not too bad actually."

"Lucky you. I reckon this stuff moonlights as paint stripper on its days off. Probably the cheapest bottle McLaren could find."

"I think there's some beer in the fridge. Why not get one of those? I'll wait here for you."

He nodded and did as she suggested.

"So, how do you know Rosemary, then?" he asked when he got back.

"Oh, I've known Rosie for years. She was actually best pals with my big sister when I was growing up. A couple of years ago I became the manager at her bank, she was a customer and we hit it off. She's a lovely girl. So honest and would do anything for you."

"Well, she'll be sorely missed around here," agreed Stark. "You can't buy her kind of care and attention. She was so nice to me when I first moved here."

Madeline raised her glass at someone behind him, and Stark instinctively looked over his shoulder. Rosemary, smiling, immediately turned back to her conversation. He looked back at Madeline, who blushed and dropped her eyes to the floor before tossing back her head and running her fingers through her glossy hair. He decided he needed to be bold.

"Listen, do you have any plans for later? Would you like to have some dinner with me?" He felt his stomach flip and his legs go to jelly as the words left his mouth. He took a swig of beer to relieve his dust-dry throat.

"Oh, well, actually, sorry but I can't."

"Ah, right, no bother," he said feeling a sickening wave of embarrassment crash over him.

"No, no, it's not that I don't want to, it's just I promised Rosie I would go out for a meal with her and her husband and my sister and a few other family and friends," she replied, touching him lightly on the arm, sending another bolt of energy through him. "Maybe another time, though?"

He felt the burning in his face subside and relief crash down like a warm shower.

"Ok, that would be great. Here's my number," he said, handing her a card.

She took it and deliberately touched his hand as she did so. They locked eyes in a gaze that felt like nothing he'd ever experienced before. She retrieved a pen from her bag and scribbled her number on the card and gave him it back. "Give me a call. Weekends are usually best for me."

He put the card back in his pocket and drained the last of his beer. "Right, great. I'll phone you tomorrow. Have a nice night with Rosemary."

Madeline leaned in and kissed him on the cheek. The smell of her perfume, the touch of her skin; he was gone. "Thanks, I will," she said and walked over to Rosemary on the other side of the room, immediately becoming engaged in an animated conversation involving lots of smiles and a hug. Stark took that as a good sign.

***

Jacobs loved driving the Porsche Boxster late at night when there was hardly anybody else on the road. It handled like a dream and went like a rocket when his heavy right foot encouraged it to. A twenty-first birthday present, it offered him a dry run for the big-time. When he got that mega-money move to the English Championship or the Scottish Premiership, this 'kid-on' Porsche would be getting traded in for the real thing; a top of the range 911. Meanwhile, the Boxster still looked the bollocks and, more importantly, it made most people around Alloa envious and admiring at the same time. Even that stupid, nosey bastard of a cop had been impressed.

He barrelled around the corner at nearly sixty miles an hour despite the greasy road surface. Most cars would have tailed out doing much more than forty-five. The g-force hauled at his still-damaged head so he eased off on the gas, cursing the bastard that caused him to fall and cut himself. When the car behind bumped him, he was still topping fifty and the Porsche went into a fishtail. Like most young men, Jacobs had a far higher opinion of his own driving ability than the facts would bear out. He'd never had an accident, never had to regain control in an emergency. He didn't know what to do and panicked, hammering the brakes and swinging the wheel around in the wrong direction. The car hit the kerb, careered back across the opposite lane and smashed through a hedge. Once through the hedge it nose-dived into a ditch and flipped onto its roof.

Inside the car, Jacobs was rocked and buffeted. The seat belt helped reduce some of the potential damage and, when the airbag deployed, he didn't get crushed by the steering column. However, going upside down brought the roof bearing down on him. Metal screamed and howled, glass shattered and plastics buckled. He felt various bones and sinews rip and break and, as the car came to halt in the ditch, he blacked out.

After a few seconds, he came to again; disorientated, pain coursing through him. However, it turned out a few damaged body parts would soon be the least of his worries. The ditch was used for drainage. As he felt the foul brown water lap against his face, he ignored the pain and released the seatbelt. The water was coming in fast through the broken driver's side window but this also offered a way out; if he could manoeuvre himself through it. He wriggled and struggled until his torso was free of the wreckage but his left leg was trapped between the seat and the crumpled dashboard. He pulled and twisted, causing searing pain to slice through his battered body once again, but it wouldn't budge.

The filthy ditch-water washed around him. His right arm was definitely broken and he needed to reach up and grab the underside of the car with his left hand to keep his head free of the water. It was exhausting and agonising; he'd never been so thankful to be as fit as he was.

Jacobs saw headlights and heard a vehicle come to a halt on the road nearby and he began to shout.

"Help! Please, help me! I've had a crash and I'm trapped. Call 999!"

He heard the thunk of the car door and tried to look up to see his saviour approaching. Nobody came running. He repeated his yelling.

He thought he heard a noise to his left and he twisted to look, causing another bout of pain to cleave through his nerve-endings. It was raining and Jacobs wondered if it had been doing so the whole time but he'd just not noticed.

Jacobs' left arm was tiring. Where was the person from the road? They must have heard him. How could they not have? He shouted for help again; desperate.

He thought about the 999 thing. Where was his mobile? He realised he'd thrown it onto the passenger seat earlier. He wouldn't be finding it any time soon.

The approaching figure was upon him before he could react. His fingers were prised loose from the underneath of the car and he dropped into the water. The shock caused him to inhale a great lungful of water and he scrabbled and hauled at the side of the car trying to regain a hold, at the same time redoubling his efforts to free his leg. He didn't understand. What were they doing? Why were they not helping him? He managed to get a hold again, spluttering and coughing, gasping as his body tried to get some oxygen into its system.

"What the..."

Again his fingers were pulled loose and again he went under. This time he managed to hold his breath before being submerged but, as he struggled to get a hold of the car's bodywork and pull himself free of the water, his tormentor stopped him. Pain pierced him like a thousand synchronised knives, his lungs burned, his vision was clouded and obscured. Why was this person doing this? Who were they? They hadn't said anything, they'd given no reason for doing this to him.

Jacobs wanted to scream for help but he couldn't afford the energy and he wasn't given enough time to gather himself to make an attempt. "Please," was all he could manage but his appeal went unheeded.

Panic took over as he realised just how serious this was getting. He'd lost the feeling in his trapped leg and it hadn't budged, despite all his struggling. Flailing about, he managed to deflect his assailant's hands and briefly gained a hold of the car; just enough to raise his head out of the water and refill his lungs with air before the attacker pulled his fingers loose and he was dunked under yet again.

He could feel his strength ebbing away. The pain, the desperation, the terror and the lack of oxygen, all combined to drain his resources. He couldn't hold his breath any longer and took in water. He knew he was done for. Two more desperate attempts to get hold of the car were thwarted and Paul Jacobs fought no more. Water inundated his lungs and he became still. The fight was over.

The bad Samaritan walked back to the road, got into the parked car, and drove away.

13.

Stark stood beside Archie Brown, the senior SOC officer, digesting the scene as one of Brown's assistants filled gigabytes of camera memory.

"Right, let's see what we've got here then, shall we?" said Brown.

He walked around the car, squatting down to check out the interior of the wrecked Porsche. He had to climb into the ditch to get a closer look at Paul Jacobs, wincing and inhaling loudly as he stepped into the frigid water. After spending a few minutes inspecting the scene, he climbed out and dictated a few notes into a hand-held digital recorder.

"Well, what are your first impressions, Archie? A straightforward accident, I presume," said Stark.

Brown shrugged and pushed out his bottom lip. "Probably. Lost control, came through the hedge and ended upside down in the ditch. His left leg seems to be lodged tight in there and it looks like he might have been trying to pull himself up the side of the car to get out of the water. My guess would be that he eventually got tired or passed out and drowned. The nails and fingertips of his left hand are mashed up but the right ones are untouched. I suspect he may have broken his right arm in the crash and couldn't use it."

"Poor bastard," said Stark. "You said *probably*, have you seen something to make you doubt that?"

"Not sure. Have a look at this," said Brown, gesturing for Stark to come around to the back of the car. "There's an unusual dent and paint mark on the back there, d'you see?"

Stark took a closer look at the area Brown was pointing

at. "Hmm, I see what you mean, right enough. You thinking he might have been involved in a collision that caused this?"

"Who knows? Maybe," replied Brown, "but it might just be long-standing damage from some other time. Seems quite fresh on first inspection, though."

Stark nodded. He walked back around the car, looking for anything unusual that might suggest foul play. He tried to remember if he'd seen any damage on the back of the car when he'd visited Jacobs but he hadn't gotten that close up to it.

"There is one other slightly odd thing," said Brown.

"What's that, then?"

"It's probably no big deal, but the keys are not in the ignition. I'm thinking maybe Jacobs took them out – he might have been worried about the engine catching fire or something like that – and then dropped them. We'll search the ditch once the car's been removed."

"Ok, that's fine," said Stark.

It was bizarre that Stark was dealing with his second drowning victim in the space of two weeks. Stranger still was that one of them had died in a ditch and the other in one of Scotland's biggest rivers. Strangest of all, that they were personally connected to each other. Then again, he'd seen weirder things during his time in London. It got him thinking of Sadie Watkins and her unorthodox approach to vigilantism. That case had taught him never to rule anything out too soon.

Stark began to walk back up the field, retracing the trajectory of the car. His feet, encased in a borrowed pair of Wellington boots, squelched and left deep impressions in the damp ground. He stopped and looked back at the footprint trail he'd left and headed back towards Brown.

"Archie, who found him an' called this in?"

"The farmer; out checking on some livestock at first light."

"Did he approach the car an' walk around it?"

"I think so, why?"

"Oh, nothing, really. Just wondered: if that bump does indicate a collision, whoever did it might have come down for a look."

"Right," said Brown, frowning.

"Well, if they did, they'd have left some footprints," said Stark.

"Oh, I see what you mean. To be honest, I don't think that's going to be easy to tell now. The farmer was on his quad bike and a few of us have been stomping about as well. Do you want us to take some casts of the footprints we *can* find?"

"I don't know. Maybe just belt an' braces. What d'you reckon yourself?"

"Alright, can't do any harm. Better to have too much evidence than not enough."

"Cheers, Archie. I'll catch up wi' you when the post mortem's ready."

"No worries, Adam. See you later."

Up on the road, the crash investigators were hard at work. A fire engine sat idling, the crew waiting to be given the nod to go down and free Paul Jacobs' body from the wreckage. Stark approached a bear of a man in a high-visibility jacket and police cap.

"How's things, Jock?"

Sergeant Jock McGinn was one of the best crash site investigators in Scotland. "Alright, Adam, I'm no' too bad, how're you doing?"

The two men shook hands.

"I'm ok, big man, thanks. Anything out of the ordinary?" asked Stark.

"No' really, mate. Looks like he hit the kerb after taking the corner too fast, an' that sent him over the carriageway, through the hedge, an' into the field. The road was wet, so there are no skid marks, but the alloys left a mark on the kerb back up the road there, eh."

"There's a dent on the back of the car. Do you think he could have been shunted?"

McGinn took a few seconds to re-survey the scene and check his notes. "Hmm, aye, maybe, I suppose. The marks on the kerb are a bit further from the corner than normal but still within possible. I did have a tiny doubt about it, given how well those cars are supposed to handle, eh. Thing is though, there's no way of telling how good or bad a driver he was, you ken what I mean? We'll need to do more detailed calculations but I suppose we shouldn't rule it out at this stage."

"I'm interested to know why it took so long for anyone to report it. It's a fairly busy road most of the time. How come nobody noticed the car through the gap in the hedge?" asked Stark.

"I think if you were coming round that corner in the dark, the angles are wrong to see beyond into the field. You might have noticed a gap in the hedge but why would you screech to a halt an' go back to see if a car was in the field? What would make you assume it was an accident that had just taken place?"

"Aye, fair point."

"It wouldn't be that busy if it happened in the early hours, which it likely did, an' it was raining. I'm no' really surprised it got overlooked until the light came up."

"Ok, that's fine, Jock. Do all the stuff you need to do an' let me know what your conclusions are. I'll see you later on. Cheers."

"Aye, no bother, Adam. Cheers."

Stark went back to his car feeling a bit uneasy about the crash. He couldn't help but think about the connection to Jonny Jacobs. Could Billy McDuff be involved? He'd heard from a friend in the prison service that Jacobs was having a hard time inside and the authorities were pretty sure McDuff was the main force behind it. Billy McDuff was a man for bearing grudges, as Stark knew all too well, and he wouldn't rule out this being some form of revenge for what happened to Billy's son. Stark hoped he was wrong and this was just an accident, plain and simple, but something nagged at his gut. He started the car and drove back towards the station to draft an initial report.

Barr nodded, "Right, but, what's that got to do wi' the crash, sir?"

Stark shrugged. "I'm no' sure, Ian. It was more than likely an accident but the dent on the back of the car got me thinking. Billy McDuff has been harassing Jonny Jacobs in the jail, making his life a misery from what I've heard. It made me wonder if he might have organised some kind of payback – eye for an eye, that sort of thing."

Barr took a moment to let this sink in. "Interesting, sir. I suppose he might have. But, like you say, Jacobs has no' exactly been Mr Popular lately. What about Frank Dawson, though? He's got good reason to be pissed off wi' Jacobs an' all, don't you think?"

Stark nodded in agreement. "Aye, I suppose he does, Ian. And who knows how many others might have been gunning for him. I wouldn't have thought this trouble wi' Dawson an' the fans is the first time he's got other folks' backs up."

"Do you think we need to look into this a bit more, sir?"

"Maybe, but let's wait for the post-mortem and big Jock's crash stuff to come in before we get too carried away. The DCI made it clear he's counting every penny, so we'll need to run it past him first, an' I'd rather have more to go on if I was doing that."

Barr grinned. "Aye, fair enough, sir."

Stark started walking away towards his desk.

"The other thing is: the connection to Colin Cook. That's his cousin an' his best pal dead within a couple of weeks. Both in suspicious circumstances. I reckon I need to have another wee chat wi' young Mr Cook."

"I reckon you do, sir."

Stark made it to his desk and sat down. He took out the card with Madeline Short's number on and looked at it. He wasn't going to get a chance to follow that particular lead up any time soon. He'd learnt from bitter experience that trying to start up a relationship with someone at the same time as being embroiled in a complex case was a bad idea. A very bad idea. Even though every fibre in his body urged him to punch her number into his mobile, he put the card back in his wallet and picked up the internal phone instead.

***

Colin Cook cancelled the call, put the mobile phone down on the table in front of him, stood up, hobbled to the bathroom and ejected his stomach contents. He washed his face and rinsed out his mouth. As he dabbed at his skin with a towel, anguish consumed him. Sitting on the bathroom floor, with his bad leg stretched out in front of him, he struggled to come to terms with this duo of hammer blows.

Sobs shuddered through him as he heard his mother's soft knock at the bathroom door.

"Are you ok, Colin?"

"No' really, Mum. I've just heard that Paul's dead." His grief produced a moan from deep inside him like nothing he remembered uttering before.

"Oh my, God! Paul? You mean Paul Jacobs? Dead? Oh, Colin, I'm so sorry. When? I mean, what happened?"

"It was a car crash. Happened last night. I don't know much else because his dad couldn't speak about it. He just phoned to let me know."

Colin heard his mother quietly weeping and blowing her nose. His parents could have papered every wall in their house with the tissues they'd used to collect the effluent of their grief.

"Are you going to be ok, son?"

"I just need a few minutes, Mum, eh."

"Ok, you know where I am if you need anything."

"Thanks, Mum."

"And Colin?"

"Aye."

"I love you, son."

"Love you too, Mum."

He heard her walk away down the stairs.

Colin and Paul were sixteen and decided it was time to experiment with alcohol. Being sporty types, they'd managed to avoid starting any earlier but, eventually, curiosity in Colin's case, and a streak of rebellion on Paul's part, got the better of them.

Colin was quite tall and already shaving. They both agreed a shopkeeper would be more inclined to believe he was eighteen than the shorter, baby-faced Paul, so he landed the task of purchasing the liquor. Being young and with limited funds, they opted for a couple of litre bottles of cheap cider.

They chose a corner shop to make their purchase as the supermarkets were a bit too hot on enforcing age restrictions. More importantly, according to the local intel, the guy who owned this particular corner shop would happily sell crack to toddlers – as long as they had the cash. Even so, Colin had never felt nerves like it. It took him half an hour of psyching himself up to go inside. He waited for the shop to empty of any other customers, grabbed the plastic bottles and put them on the counter. The guy asked for the money and sent him on his way with barely a glance in his direction.

Carrier bag in hand, they made for the railway bridge across the then-disused line, feeling like the kings of the universe; bravado and bullshit oozed from every orifice. Once they were safely out of view, in amongst the remnants of other people's illicit imbibing and bodily fluids, they got stuck into their contraband. By the time they'd finished, Paul was in some state. Colin seemed to have a far higher tolerance for alcohol than his companion, managing to maintain enough coherence to escort the almost comatose Paul home. However, despite Colin's best efforts to sober him up, Paul stumbled into his house, crashed into the front room, puked on his dog and collapsed in front of his horrified parents. Colin made good his escape and managed to avoid any such indignities back at his own house.

He laughed out loud thinking of the poor dog and what a shock it must have been for it. He burst out crying as he thought of how empty he felt; like all his internal organs had been removed for transplant without his consent.

The weight of his guilt flattened him to the floor, preventing his muscles from functioning as they should. Something very bad was happening and the more he dwelt on it, the more he felt he deserved it.

It didn't matter how sorry he was.

It was too late for sorry.

Sorry would never be enough.

***

Jonny Jacobs couldn't see properly. Every fully-functioning nerve ending appeared to be preoccupied with delivering excruciating pain to all parts of his body. It was really bad down his arm and in his chest. The call from his brother Sam delivered a crushing blow to his resolve, to his motivation to struggle on. Only the final words of his stricken wife as she faded away were harder for him to deal with than this. Paul was dead and Jonny would never get the chance to make it up to the boy for letting him down so badly. He'd never see him rise to the top of the football tree, never even speak to him again. His brother had been destroyed and Jonny was no use to him, no support, no comfort. It was worse than that, though. The brutal truth was, he was making things worse, multiplying the grief.

The hero of no-one.

Pain flooded through him now, like whatever synaptic dam had been holding the worst of it back just burst.

The prison officer keeping an eye on Jacobs didn't have to be psychic to know something was very badly amiss with his charge. He made the call for help as Jacobs fell to the floor, moaning.

Three officers took turns trying to revive Jonny Jacobs but by the time the paramedics arrived, he was beyond even their skills. The officers knew about the rumours but they'd done their job. The one who'd been looking after Jonny didn't believe the gossip. He'd been a huge fan as a kid, with posters on his wall and even a signed programme still secreted somewhere in a drawer. He knew someone who'd been at the trial and heard the evidence, and none of it referred to abuse – sexual or otherwise. All of them had done their best but it was never going to be enough to save Jonny Jacobs from his broken heart.

14.

Stark talked the situation through with McLaren, trying to decide on how best to proceed with a burgeoning workload. Chief among their decisions was to bring in DI Jim McGhee from Stirling to help. Stark and McGhee worked together very effectively during the McDuff case and gained huge amounts of mutual respect in that time. Given the cutbacks, and the scale of the evidence trail, it would be impossible to do it without help – it might as well be someone they both knew and respected. McLaren would do his usual frontman act as far as the media was concerned.

The gathered throng included nearly all the personnel they had at their disposal. A buzz of excitement hung in the air. These types of mass assemblages only ever took place when things got juicy in a policing sense. McLaren brought the meeting to order.

"Right folks, we've got you all together to discuss a couple of ongoing investigations that appear to be converging an' are developing at a pace. I'm going to hand the floor over to DI Stark now, who'll be leading these investigations along wi' our colleague DI Jim McGhee from Stirling; who some of you will already know."

Stark took a while talking through the different strands of the case as it stood. The Cook girl's apparent suicide; the texts sent to her cousin from her phone, post her death; the mystery car driver who failed to help Colin Cook after almost running him over; the connection to Paul Jacobs whose death had not been confirmed as accidental yet; and the birdwatcher who took photos of the dead girl after he found her. It was a lot to take in and there were a number of questions to clarify points throughout.

"This could get quite involved an' intense. We've got a prominent local family involved here, an' a footballer with a colourful past. The press are going to go for this big time if we confirm either or both of these deaths as suspicious. Please, an' I know you've heard it all before, but please don't discuss this wi' anyone from the media. We need to agree our party line first an' none of us want to spend less time dealing with these cases because we're too busy fielding press enquiries, ok?"

There was the general hubbub of inferred assent. Even McLaren nodded in an approving way.

"Would you like to say anything else, sir?" asked Stark, turning to his boss.

"Aye, just to say, let's try an' get this sorted out quickly an' wi' the minimum of fuss. Like DI Stark says, let's keep this out of the press until we're ready to deal wi' them. Good luck."

The room began to clear, leaving the three-man CID team to dish out tasks between them.

Stark flicked through his notes, trying to make sure they were covering all the ground they needed to.

"Jim, we'll need to check an' see if we've had the report back from big Jock yet."

"It's top of my list to track down, Adam," replied McGhee.

"Nice one. Ian, did we get the PM back on Jacobs?"

"I think it came in just before the meeting, it should be waiting in your email for you."

"Right, but have *you* looked at it?" asked Stark, his patience straining under Barr's unusual display of apathy.

"No, sir, it came in literally a minute before this meeting. I didn't have enough time, eh."

Stark shook his head. He knew it wasn't really Barr's fault. After all, he'd got the email as well and hadn't looked at it – but it was more the tone of the reply, rather than its substance, that irked him.

"Jim, we'll go an' have a look at that in a minute. It could have a big effect on how both of us proceed."

Stark opened the email containing Archie Brown's report. The main findings were unsurprising – Paul Jacobs drowned in the ditch. There were various injuries that could be attributed to the crash such as a broken left leg, broken right arm, and the contusions and abrasions on his left hand and arm from the apparent attempt to save himself. Nothing unusual or worrying leapt out at either cop. The only slight oddity was that the keys had not been recovered at the scene. Brown hypothesised about them being buried in the mud of the ditch and wondered how thorough a search they should conduct, how relevant their absence was. Stark wasn't too sure himself but it was an anomaly to keep in mind.

As they finished reading, the preview dialogue box for an email from Jock McGinn appeared on the screen. Stark raised his eyebrows at McGhee and opened it. They read through it together.

"Right, that's that settled then. We need to talk to Colin Cook. Something is beginning to smell bad, Jim. I don't know exactly what, but there are some rather implausible coincidences happening here."

"I would be inclined to agree wi' you there, Adam."

"It could be a simple accident. Whoever bumped him just panicked an' left the scene without realising how serious it was."

"That's one explanation, certainly."

"Then again, maybe they'd been drinking an' couldn't face the music; just hoped Jacobs would be alright or would be found by someone else?"

"Again, I can't fault the logic."

"Thing is though, Jim, I can't shake this feeling that it's more than that. Something deliberate. He's been a bad lad in his time, noised up a few folks. It's likely they didn't mean to kill him but I have a strong feeling they meant to teach him a lesson," said Stark.

"Yeah, he does come across as a bit of an arrogant wee shite from the stuff I've read about him in the papers, an' interviews on the telly," replied McGhee.

"You know he's Jonny Jacobs' nephew an' all, don't you?"

"Aye, an' I suppose you've been thinking about whether the McDuffs might have been involved an' all – tit for tat sort of thing?"

"It crossed my mind, Jim. We'll need to talk to them at some point I would imagine but let's start wi' the Cook laddie."

"Lead on Mc … ha, only kidding!"

Both men laughed as they made their way out to the car park.

"You want to talk about Paul? Why? It was a car crash. What do you need to know from me about that?" said Colin. His escalating anxiety caused a marked increase in his fidgeting.

"Look, there's no easy way to tell you this, son. We think Paul was the victim of a hit an' run. Somebody shunted him off the road."

"Oh, no! No, no, no. Fuck, fuck, fuck! This can't be happening."

It was hard to tell if Margo Cook's horrified expression was caused by the bad news or by her son's foul-mouthed outburst. "Oh, God," was all she managed to say.

"I understand how hard this must be for you to take in, Colin, especially so soon after Debbie's death, but I need to get to the bottom of any connections – if there are any."

McGhee and Stark gave the Cooks a moment or two to compose themselves. Stark sipped at his tea. It was rank – weak, insipid and with sugar added. He put it back down and left it to go cold.

"Can you think of anyone who might have held a

grudge against Paul Jacobs, or wished him ill?" asked Stark.

"How long have you got?" said Colin, the humour barely noticeable, the smile beyond weak. "He could be difficult. He had a high opinion of himself, which was mostly justified. Paul was the best at most sports, did well in exams, always had the best looking girls, eh. People were jealous an' bitter an' he would take pleasure rubbing their noses in it."

"Sounds like a great guy," muttered McGhee.

The Cook boy bristled, colour returning to his face. "Aye, he *was* a great fuckin guy actually!"

"Colin, please," hissed Margo.

"You didn't know him like I did, like Debbie did. Paul would do anything for his mates, eh. He just took no shit, that's all. He was on the phone right away, took me out for a beer, tried to help me deal wi' what happened. Then … " His fire burned out and the struggle to contain his emotions gripped him again.

"Ok, fair enough. Thing is, I can't help wondering whether Paul and Debbie's deaths might be connected. Is there any reason somebody might want to harm both of them?" asked Stark.

Colin rocked, elbows on his knees, moving his hands across his scalp. Tears dropped to the floor and he sniffed, mumbling, "No, no, there's nobody. Nobody. Nobody … there's nobody left."

"Just for the record, Colin. Where were you last night between the hours of eleven pm and four am?"

"He was here, at home, in bed," said Margo Cook. "He fell running and hurt his ankle and was in bed early with some painkillers. I hope you're not inferring anything DI Stark?" Her face was pink, her tone clipped.

"No, not at all, I'm just putting as much information into the pot as possible, Mrs Cook."

"Well, I don't like your tone. The idea that he had anything to do with what happened to Paul is an insult and totally absurd!" she shouted.

Colin's shoulders heaved and his sobs became louder. His mother put her arms around him and soothed him. Stark looked at McGhee, who nodded. They wrapped things up and made their way back to the car.

"What do you think?" asked McGhee.

"Hmm, I'm no' sure, Jim. I can't see the Cook lad having anything to do wi' it. His grief's too genuine … if he's at it, he's a bloody good actor."

"Yeah, I agree. Still, something's not right, eh. Something's just not quite fitting together. Only, I can't quite get a grip on it yet."

"Exactly how I feel," replied Stark. "Let's go and see Jacobs' dad. I want to let him know what's happened an' I want to see if he'll let us search the boy's flat. I don't really know what I'm looking for but there might be some kind of lead to be had there."

"That sounds like a good idea to me, mate."

15.

"Shit, ok, thanks," said Stark putting his phone back in his pocket.

"What's up?" asked McGhee.

"Apparently, Jonny Jacobs is dead. Took a heart attack when he heard the news about Paul."

"Jeezo, that's not good. I dunno, I always thought he was a decent guy who got desperate an' did something stupid, rather than a genuine wrong 'un, eh."

"Unlike Malky McDuff," said Stark.

"Indeed. Jacobs' brother might no' be too receptive to our visit now, though. Son an' brother gone a day after each other is going to be pretty tough to deal with."

"Aye, poor bastard. The problem is, I don't want him hearing about the cause of Paul's accident from somebody else. I think we need to at least go around there and tell him that. If he's in no fit state to answer any questions, we'll leave it an' come back after. What do you think, Jim?"

"Sounds reasonable to me, Adam. I think you're right about getting the story from us an' no' from one of the boy's mates or, worse, some bloody journalist."

Sam Jacobs' home was an impressive pile of masonry. Not quite the palatial proportions of Grant Cook's house, but close enough. There were five cars tightly parked together in the driveway, which suggested visitors bringing sympathy and support. Stark wished that was all he was bringing with him.

"Yes?" asked the teenage girl who answered the door; eyes and nose reddened with grief.

"Hello, we're police officers, I was looking for Mr Jacobs. Is he in?" said Stark, holding up his warrant card for the girl to see.

"Is this about Paul?" she asked, her voice wavering.

"I'd rather talk to Mr Jacobs if that's ok, Miss. Can you tell him we're here please?"

She turned and headed back inside, leaving the door ajar. The two policemen could hear the gentle murmur of voices coming from within and the smell of home baking wafted towards them. Stark felt his stomach grumble in response to the aroma. It only took a few seconds for Sam Jacobs to appear at the door. He looked how Stark thought he might – a fully-clothed shadow.

"Alright? What's this all about? My niece said you need to talk to me," he said, his voice no more substantial than his demeanour.

"Yes, that's right Mr Jacobs. I'm Detective Inspector Adam Stark and this is Detective Inspector Jim McGhee. Is there somewhere we can talk to you in private?"

"Not really, we've got visitors. It's not a good time."

"I appreciate that, sir. I'm aware of what's happened and I'm very sorry for your loss. However, there's something you need to know about the circumstances surrounding your son's death that I'd rather you heard from us than elsewhere."

Stark saw Jacobs wilt, gripping the door handle for support. "You better come in. We can use my study."

They followed him through the wide hallway, up a flight of stairs and into a room that in most houses would have been a decent-sized master bedroom. It was kitted out as any home office might be, the walls adorned with framed pictures of family and pets; quite a few of them recording Paul Jacobs' sporting achievements.

"So, what is it you need to tell me, detective?" asked Jacobs.

"I'm afraid there's no easy way to tell you this, Mr Jacobs, but we think your son may have been run off the road," said Stark.

Jacobs let out a low moan, staggered and sat in the

chair next to his desk. He put his face in his hands, muttering denials.

"We haven't got much to go on at the minute and, so far, nobody has come forward as a witness. We'd like to ask you a few questions if you feel able to answer them."

Jacobs sat back in the seat and let his hands fall onto his knees, shrugged and nodded. "What do you want to know?"

"Do you know if Paul was worried about anything or anyone? Did he have any enemies you were aware of?"

"Paul was my son and I loved him but he could be a little shit. He rubbed people up the wrong way a lot of the time. He never worried what people thought of him – he was fearless. It's what helped to make him such a good footballer. I don't know of any enemies, well, proper ones. Ones who would try to … kill him." Jacobs looked up to the ceiling, sucked in air and battled to stay in control.

"Ok, that's fine. It's not definite he was deliberately killed. We can't rule out it just being an accident; someone who panicked an' left the scene out of fear of the consequences."

"A drunk, you mean," said Jacobs, bitterness soaking his words.

"Maybe," said Stark, "or a youngster."

Sam Jacobs seemed like a reasonable, rational man, coping remarkably well considering what he was going through. Stark decided to chance his luck.

"I wonder, Mr Jacobs, if you have access to Paul's flat?"

"Yes, I have a key. Why?"

"I'd like to go an' have a look, see if I can find anything that might help lead me to a suspect."

Jacobs stood. "Wait here. I'll go and get it."

Once he'd left the room, Stark turned to McGhee. "God, this is brutal."

"Aye, he's a broken man, an' no wonder. This is a hellish situation. What did you say you were after in the flat, by the way?"

"I really don't know. Just think it's worth a look."

"Fair enough," said McGhee, as Sam Jacobs returned with the key.

"Here you go," he said, handing it over to Stark.

"Thanks. I'll bring it back as soon as I can."

"My wife blames me, you know," said Jacobs.

"Sorry?" replied Stark.

"I bought him that bloody Porsche."

"Oh, right, I see. Well, I don't suppose it makes it any better but I don't think the type of car would have made much difference. It was a severe impact and very bad luck to have ended up in that ditch," said Stark, McGhee nodding in agreement.

"Is there anything else, detective inspector? It's just that I've got guests and I'll need to let my wife know about this. She's not doing so well."

"No, I think that's all we need for now, Mr Jacobs," said Stark and both he and McGhee handed over cards with encouragement to use them if he thought of anything relevant.

They made their way back down the stairs. As they stepped out of the house, Stark stopped and turned back before Jacobs could close the door.

"Sorry, there is one more thing, Mr Jacobs. I was wondering whether you were aware of any threats made by the McDuffs towards you or Paul or your brother?"

Colour flushed into Sam Jacobs' face and his voice rose well above the croaky mumble he'd managed so far. "Are they behind this? Those fucking animals?" He fashioned as deep a frown as Stark had ever seen. "I've just realised – you're the cop who arrested Jonny. You were in court for the trial. I thought I knew you from somewhere. Are you telling me you think they might have had something to do with Paul ... and Jonny?"

"No, look, Mr Jacobs, I didn't say that. I just want to make sure we're investigating every avenue. As far as I know, your brother had a heart attack in his cell. I can't see how any of the McDuffs could have been responsible for that," countered Stark.

"No, I don't suppose you can, DI Stark. Just like you couldn't see how Jonny had been bullied and manipulated into kidnapping that kid. How desperate he was. Wait, I notice you didn't deny they could have killed Paul, though."

Stark was rattled. Jacobs was riled and tack-sharp. Stark needed to regain control of the interview. As he tried to formulate some kind of appeasement, a striking-looking woman appeared at Jacobs' shoulder.

"Sam, what's going on? What are you shouting about?" she asked.

Jacobs was thrown off his stride, his anger deflating as if pricked by a pin. "I'm sorry, darling, I just got a bit upset. They're police and, I'm afraid to say, they brought more bad news. Let's go upstairs so I can tell you about it," he said softly, putting his arm around her shoulders. He stared at the two cops as he began closing the door over. "I'll be in touch, DI Stark."

Back in the car, McGhee spoke first.

"That didn't go quite how you'd hoped, then."

"No, it bloody didn't. I should have left the McDuff stuff until later, when things weren't so raw. I didn't expect him to be so quick, though. Did you notice how he picked me up on the Paul and Jonny thing?"

"I certainly did! He could get a job with us any day. What does he do, by the way?"

"No' sure, to be honest. I remember him, now, from the courtroom, but he was never called as a witness when I was there; he was just sitting in the public gallery. I'll find out, though. We're going to have to watch our step around him. Anyway, let's go over to the flat an' see if we can turn anything up," said Stark, starting the car.

"You sure you don't want to go via the pub, get a wee half for your nerves?" said McGhee, smirking.

"Piss off," said Stark and drove off, thinking it wasn't actually such a bad idea.

The door pushed back a small pile of mail as Stark and McGhee entered the flat. Stark scooped it up and flicked through it, looking for anything interesting. It was mainly circulars and adverts, along with an electricity bill and an invitation to apply for a credit card. The same detritus he could expect to build up behind his own door if he left his house unattended for a couple of days. He dropped them onto the kitchen counter.

"Let's not make the place look like it's been burgled for the moment, Jim. We'll have a sweep of everything obvious without ripping open the upholstery or suchlike, ok?"

"Well, seeing as we don't actually know what we're looking for, that seems like a sensible approach, Adam."

"You try the bedroom and bathroom. I'll look in here an' the living room."

McGhee nodded and walked off toward the bathroom.

Stark looked along the worktops, opened cupboards and even looked in the oven, although, as he was doing it, he couldn't imagine any scenario in which that might have been likely to turn up any kind of useful lead. *Yes, sir, it was amazing. I opened the oven and there it was - the threatening letter the suspect sent to Jacobs just before his death!* After a few minutes he'd found nothing to pique his interest. It wasn't a big room and it didn't take long. He made his way into the front room.

Stark stood in the middle of the room looking around but nothing jumped out at him. He walked over to the window and looked out into the street. A few parked cars, a man walking his dog in the rain. All normal. He turned back to begin searching when McGhee called him through to the bedroom.

"Aye, what've you got, Jim?"

McGhee pointed to the bedside table. An iPhone sat

118

next to a radio alarm clock. It was in a blinged-up case, encrusted with a mixture of pink and silver faux diamonds.

"Ok. Looks a bit girly for a macho footballer, don't you think?" said Stark.

"Exactly what I was thinking," replied McGhee, raising his eyebrows. "Did Jacobs have a girlfriend?"

"I'm no' sure, Jim. He never mentioned a partner an' there was no lassie here when I came round last time. Is there any sign of cosmetics or toiletries suggesting a girl stays here – even if it's only now an' again?"

"Nope. Just shaving gear, deodorant, shower gel, that sort of thing. All masculine packaging an' brands, eh."

"So, if he's no' living wi' anyone, why would he have a girl's iPhone in his bedroom?"

"A one-night-stand left it behind?" mused McGhee.

"Could be that, right enough. Something odd about it, though, don't you think? My first thought was those texts to Colin "Coco" Cook."

"Ok. You think it could be the Cook lassie's phone?"

"Well, I'm no' definite, obviously, but Jacobs' attitude towards her death was cold, dismissive, you know? She was supposed to be one of his oldest friends but he wasn't exactly grief-stricken."

"Right, well, you better switch it on; see if it is hers."

Stark picked up the phone, turning it over in his gloved hand as he did so. He pressed the circular button on the front but nothing happened. He pushed the power button on the top but, again, nothing happened.

"Bollocks. Out of juice or busted. Do you have an iPhone, Jim?"

McGhee snorted. "Naw. I'm about as big a technophobe as you're ever going to meet. I thought you might have had one yourself though, Adam?"

"Nah, I'm no' a big fan, actually. Too expensive an' too fragile for my liking. I had one a while back but I was shitting it the whole time in case I lost it or broke it. You know what it's like in this job – you end up in all sorts of scrapes an' capers. I can't see a charger anywhere obvious, so we'll take it back to the office. Somebody's bound to have one we can borrow," said Stark, dropping the lifeless phone into an evidence bag and stuffing it into his pocket. "Anything else catch your eye?"

"No' really, Adam. I think we should leave it for now. See what the score is wi' the phone an' come back for a proper search if we need to."

"Yep. That sounds like a plan. I tell you what, though. If this is Debbie Cook's phone … shits an' fans spring to mind."

McGhee shook his head as they locked up. "You're no' kidding, Adam."

16.

Stark took the charger he'd borrowed from Jane in reception and plugged it into the wall. It would take a few minutes to get enough power into the phone to start it up. As he sat at his desk, Ian Barr knocked on his door.

"Excuse me, sir. You got a minute?"

"Aye, come in, Ian. Grab a pew."

Barr sat down and took out his notebook and phone. He looked a bit fed up.

"I wanted to let you know that we've interviewed all the pals we have contact details for and nobody has given us anything to go on. Sorry."

"Naw, naw, that's fine. It's no' that surprising, really. Anyway, it might no' matter, now."

"What do you mean, sir?

"We've found a lassie's mobile in Jacobs' flat. I'm waiting for it to charge up to see whose it is," said Stark pointing to the phone lying on his desk.

Stark saw the gloom lift and the light bulb go off in Barr's head – much as it had in his. "Debbie Cook's phone?"

"Well, that's what I thought but we can't get too carried away until we make sure. In the meantime, I want you to take a couple of the PCs an' go over to Jacobs' block of flats, do a door-to-door. I want to know if anyone's seen him acting weird, anyone hanging about they didn't recognise. You know the script."

"Ok, sir. You mean now?"

"Err, that's right, I mean now, Ian."

Barr practically jumped out of his seat and scampered out of the office. Stark couldn't help but smile.

There were twenty-four flats in the block, spread over six floors. Barr sent PC Connelly and PC McKay up to the top while he started on the ground floor. He didn't see the point in having a dog and barking yourself. He rang the bell of the first door but after three attempts, no-one answered. The door to the second flat gleamed with a new coat of black, gloss paint. He could practically see his reflection in it. A coarse-fibred welcome mat awaited visitors. It's condition suggested either a lack of use or an obsessive level of cleanliness on the part of the owner. The brass nameplate revealed the householder to be a MRS. M. CAMPBELL and the doorbell chimed with a slow, satisfying and nostalgic *biiing* ... *booooong* ...

He heard her approach the door and stop – he presumed this was in order to use the spyhole. "Hello? Can I help you?" came the voice from behind the door. A strong, confident tone in a local accent.

"Mrs Campbell? My name is Detective Constable Ian Barr." He held up his warrant card for her to inspect from behind her wooden shield. "I wonder if you wouldn't mind helping me wi' some enquiries?"

He heard her put the chain on the door before opening it. "Can I see your identification, please?"

Barr handed her the card. He was impressed by her caution; too many trusting old folks were taken advantage of by charlatans. She took a few seconds to examine it before returning it to him with a thank you, unhooking the chain and opening the door wide. "Come in, son?"

He wiped his feet and stepped into the hallway.

Mrs Campbell was small, dressed all in black, with a tightly-wound bun of snow white hair on top of her head. She wore dark-rimmed glasses on a string and walked with a stick. A hand-crafted wooden one, as opposed to a standard-issue NHS job. The flat smelt of roses and lavender. Photos of people, particularly children, abounded. Barr felt like he'd stepped into another world from a bygone age, a museum maybe. But this was no dusty, fusty shrine to the past. It was elegant, beautifully maintained and welcoming. If that beer company made grannies, then they'd probably have made her.

She led him to the lounge and prompted him to sit on the couch. "Would you like a cup of tea, son?"

"Not unless you were making one for yourself anyway, Mrs Campbell, eh."

"It's no bother. What do you take?"

"Well, ok, ta. Just black, please." Barr was of the same opinion as his wife, Kirsty. Most people made bloody awful tea if you gave them the option of adding milk. It was better to avoid embarrassment all round.

She returned with a tray and set it down on the coffee table between them. With drinks poured, and the first sip taken, Barr began his questions.

"I don't know if you're aware, Mrs Campbell, but your neighbour, Mr Jacobs, in flat twelve, was killed in a road traffic accident a couple of nights ago."

She shook her head. "No, son. I didn't know that. That's a terrible shame. He was so young. Played football, I think."

"Aye, that's right, he did. Anyway, we're pretty sure it was a straightforward accident but we're just trying to see if we can find out anything that might help us in our enquiries. Did you know Mr Jacobs well?"

Again, she shook her head. "No' really, son. He wasn't awful friendly, to tell you the truth. I bumped into him a few times in the passing but he barely even said hello. He never caused me any bother though, you ken, but I know the wee woman underneath him used to moan about his loud music."

"Right. I wonder if you noticed anything unusual in the past few weeks or days? Anything he was doing that was out of the ordinary, strangers hanging about, that sort of thing."

She took a sip of her tea and seemed to drift for a moment. "Actually, you know what, there was something odd happened a few days ago. I heard the clatter of footsteps on the stairs. Somebody in a real hurry. I happened to be standing over at the window, watching the world go by – as you do when you've got a lot of time on your hands, you ken?" Barr nodded. Nothing about this warm, well-mannered woman suggested she was curtain-twitcher or a tittle-tattle merchant. "Well, all of a sudden, the Jacobs laddie comes rushing out the close, and starts running up the street. Then this car suddenly screeched away from the pavement and then he ran back, jumped in that sports car of his and drove off like a bat out of hell. After a few minutes he came back and went back into his flat."

Barr scribbled some notes and took a sip of the tea. "That's really interesting, Mrs Campbell. Did you happen to see what kind of car it was he chased after?"

"Well, I'm no' really an expert on cars, son. It was black, very shiny. One of those jeep thingies, you ken? One of those big, what do they call them, four-by-fours?"

"That's grand, I don't suppose you saw the registration?" asked Barr, not hopeful of a positive answer.

"No. I don't … oh no, wait, I remember it was short, just a few letters. I don't remember what they were but it wasn't like an ordinary number plate."

"Have you seen the car since then at all?"

"No, son, but, to be fair, I wouldn't have been looking for it especially," she said smiling.

"Ok, Mrs Campbell. You've been incredibly helpful. If you think of anything else, please give me a call," he said, handing her his card.

They exchanged pleasantries and she saw him to the door. The rest of the interviews passed without any corroboration of the incident described by Mrs Campbell or anything more of note. Most of the other people who were home were indifferent or unimpressed by Jacobs' approach to being a neighbour. None of them were in mourning.

Stark retrieved a copy of the local paper from the reception area. As he waited for the phone to come back to life, he read the coverage about Paul Jacobs. It was fair to say it was high on drama but lacking in heartfelt emotion. They speculated on the cause of the accident, thinking mechanical failure or driver error to be most likely to blame. They had a few vague platitudes from ex-team mates and a couple of fans with little or nothing in the way of affection, loss or sympathy contained within them. When he'd finished with it, Stark dropped the paper into Jim McGhee's lap.

"There you go. Have a little look at that."

"Anything worth reading?" asked McGhee.

"No' really. He's no' going to be missed by many from what I can tell. One thing I did notice was a picture of that Frank Dawson."

McGhee looked puzzled.

"You know, the team captain, the one Jacobs is supposed to have had a bust-up with?" prompted Stark.

"Oh, aye. I mind that, now. You mentioned it in the initial briefing."

"That's it. Well, it turns out he's got a broken leg and, from the looks of the photo in there, he's still in plaster."

"Would make running Jacobs off the road a wee bit of a challenge, then," said McGhee.

"Exactly. I think we can rule him out as a suspect for now. Let's not waste time interviewing him unless we get desperate."

McGhee agreed. "So, this phone, then. Will it be charged up enough to start?"

Stark unhooked it from the cable and pressed the power button. "Moment of truth."

The logo appeared as expected and the phone went into its tedious start-up rigmarole. Stark thought it odd how his patience and sense of time were different when it came to technology. Something about it made you expect instant gratification at all times – despite all your experience to the contrary. Eventually, the lock screen appeared. A picture of a cat playing the piano. Nothing specific. Nothing to help identify the owner. He slid the unlock bar across.

"Bollocks!"

"What?"

"We need the bloody pass code to open it."

"Eh?"

"Like a pin number. It stops anyone apart from the owner being able to use the phone. Whoever owns it has set a pass code. Trust them to be so security conscious. I never bothered my arse wi' one. Too annoying having to put it in every time I looked at it," said Stark, placing the phone back in an evidence bag. "Oh well, we'll just need to hand this over to the tech guys to crack."

"Erm, I know I'm no' the most technically gifted guy ever, Adam, but would it no' be quite easy to find out if it's Debbie Cook's phone without doing that?" asked McGhee.

"How do you mean?"

"Well, we could phone her number, an' if it rings, then it's hers," said McGhee, turning up both palms and shrugging.

"Oh, for fuck's sake, of course!" said Stark, feeling his face warm to his embarrassment. It was definitely possible to over-think these things. Stark opened a file on his computer and scrolled through to the number. He took out his own phone and punched in the required digits. "Here goes," he said as he pressed call.

It took about three seconds before the screen lit up and the iPhone in the bag responded with some bland pop song Stark didn't recognise for a ringtone.

"Shits and fans … " said McGhee.

It was seven o'clock and Stark should have gone home over an hour ago. DCI McLaren sat in his chair, listening to Stark and McGhee update him on the Cook and Jacobs situation. When they'd finished, he clasped his hands behind his head and let out a long sigh. "Oh, good. So he killed her, stole her phone and harassed his best friend with it. What a truly lovely young gentleman he was."

"It looks that way, sir. The thing is, even if he did kill Debbie Cook, we're short of a confession, an' without that, we'll no' be able to prove anything for certain," said Stark.

"No, an' that's probably no' going to be good enough for Grant Cook." McLaren stood up and looked out of his office window.

"I'm no' sure Sam Jacobs is going to be too impressed either, sir. I don't see him being too happy about us calling his son a killer without any other evidence than the phone. To be fair, it's possible Jacobs acquired the phone somehow without killing Debbie Cook."

McLaren and McGhee both snorted. "Seems pretty unlikely, don't you think, Stark?" said the DCI.

"Unlikely, aye, but we've no way of proving it one hundred percent one way or another now."

The three men dropped into contemplative silence. Tension crackled between and around them as if they'd wandered into the middle of a Van de Graaff generator.

"The other fly in the ointment is the crash," said Stark, breaking first. "Sam Jacobs will expect us to find out who ran his son off the road and, to be fair, even if he was an unpleasant wee turd who murdered his friend, we should."

McGhee nodded. "Adam's right, sir. If whoever did that gets away wi' it, we'll no' be doing our jobs right, ch."

McLaren retook his seat and fiddled with a pen. "Right, let's get our stories straight here before I go to the media or the Chief wi' anything. We tell them we have strong reason to believe Debbie Cook's death wasn't suicide, that we are pursuing a solid line of enquiry; we have a suspect but can't name them for now for procedural reasons. Yes?"

McGhee and Stark nodded.

"Ok, I'll sort out that press conference. Separately,

Stark, you put out an appeal for witnesses regarding the death of Paul Jacobs."

Again they agreed.

"Fine. For now, we take the same vague line wi' Grant Cook an' Sam Jacobs as we are wi' the media. We don't need them at each other's throats about this or blabbing to the press, trying to make their own case. What are you two planning on doing next?"

"I think we need to do a proper search of Paul Jacobs' flat. Tomorrow we need to tear it up; look for anything that might help prove how or why he killed Debbie Cook," said Stark. "If Debbie Cook *was* pushed off the Clacks bridge by Jacobs, he'd have had to take her there in a car. Unfortunately, that car has been totalled and dipped in a ditch but I'll ask Archie to give it another once over; look for signs she was in it."

McGhee took over. "We also need to talk to the McDuffs. If the collision wi' Jacobs car was deliberate, they're prime candidates to have been involved."

"Aye, ok, agreed. That all makes sense. Let's get on wi' this tomorrow an' get it put to bed as soon as possible," concluded McLaren, dismissing them for the evening.

***

Stark sat and stared at the half empty whisky bottle. He knew it was a pointless act, that oblivion wasn't the real answer. He knew he was risking a whole different set of problems if he kept at this but, somehow, he couldn't muster the enthusiasm to avoid it. His card with Madeline Short's number scrawled on it slipped into his peripheral vision, trying to pull him away from the bottle, taunting him to act, to find the courage to call. He slurped down a slug of whisky, feeling it burn and soothe, and pushed the card around with his fingertip. His promise to phone her the day after the leaving do had already been broken. The longer he left it the more awkward it would get, the less enthusiastic he would appear, and the less likely she would be to say yes when he did get around to it.

Stark so wanted to call but he knew nothing good could come of trying to start up a meaningful relationship in the midst of this shit storm.

He got up and went over to his stereo, looking for solace or escape in a tune. He ran his eye back and forth along the lines of CD spines, searching for an answer. He'd always favoured loud rock music, something with guitars that kicked in your teeth while melting your heart but, in recent years, a mellowing had allowed quieter, less visceral stuff to creep into the alphabetised ranks. He settled on *Brad*, an offshoot of *Pearl Jam* with laid-back guitars and soulful vocals, and returned to his seat.

The bank manageress wasn't the only one imploring him. He felt the impatient glare of Debbie Cook upon him.

Stark wondered why Jacobs might have killed her. There was no indication of anything sexual having occurred; no obvious physical assault of any kind took place prior to her falling, or being pushed, into the water. It was one of the most compelling arguments for suicide. Why would she have climbed over the barrier? How did he persuade her to jump? Maybe he had a weapon, she hedged her bets, chose to jump but lost the gamble? There were drugs involved but Archie Brown told him the amount in her system wasn't sufficient to cause her to lose consciousness. He didn't like it, it didn't feel right. Something was off-kilter. The phone bothered him too. Why would Jacobs torment Colin Cook? What motive could he have for that? Being an obnoxious, arrogant shithouse wasn't enough. It was too sadistic, cruel, calculated.

Jacobs' death had well and truly buggered things up, left them with so many unanswered and potentially unanswerable questions. Two families driven mad with guilt, hatred and uncertainty; a hostile, sneering media;

unimpressed superior officers; and, blood-boiling levels of frustration for him and McGhee.

Fill glass.
Drain.
Repeat.
Add nausea.

17.

Colin Cook watched McLaren and then Stark deliver their pieces to camera on the lunchtime news. His ankle was still nagging him but he didn't really need that excuse to stay away from work – being employed by his father meant he could get away with taking as much compassionate leave as he needed. He'd barely left the house for three days.

The cops had been vague. He knew it was deliberate and he wanted to know what they knew. He wanted to know who this suspect was. He wanted to find out who'd run into the back of Paul and sent him through the hedge to his death. He wanted all of this madness to stop, to wake up and find out he'd been tripping or dreaming.

It wasn't just the recent past that was dominating his thoughts. He was going further back, to times they'd all agreed never to talk about; never to discuss again. A time of regrets and remorse, of secrets to be kept at all costs. Only now, he reckoned they were paying the price.

***

Stark and McGhee arrived at Cammy McDuff's place shortly before one o'clock. Knocking at the door failed to elicit any response from the young householder. There was a customised, purple Citroen Saxo sitting in the driveway – just the type of car Stark imagined the boy to have. Cheap to run and easy to pimp. Stark walked around it looking for any signs of damage. It was immaculate, not a scratch on it. He radioed the details in to be checked. McDuff might have a millionaire for a mother but that wouldn't guarantee he stuck to the law as far as tax and insurance was concerned.

"Let's just wait in the car for him. Amazingly, it seems like he's up an' away bright an' early this morning."

"Or he's lying comatose in his scratcher an' can't be arsed answering the door," said McGhee, pointing to the closed curtains in the upstairs front room.

"Hmm," said Stark and walked back up the drive. He hammered on the door, rang the bell, hammered again and yelled for Cammy to wake up and answer. After three rounds of this, the curtains were prised open a fraction and he saw the bleary face of the McDuff boy scowling down at him. The lad shook his head and the curtains closed again. Stark repeated his hammer, ring and shout routine.

The door burst open to reveal a half-dressed, dishevelled Cammy McDuff, "Alright, alright. Give us a fuckin' chance will you? What do you want?"

"Hello, Cammy, we'd like a wee word wi' you, son. Can we come in?" said Stark.

McDuff sighed. "Ok, but I've done fuck all."

Stark and McGhee chuckled as they entered the house. Having cleared a place to sit, Stark began to question the lad.

"This is a nice place, or at least it would be if you kept it clean. Jesus, Cammy, you're no' too big on the housework now, are you?"

McDuff just tutted and shook his head, playing with a pack of cigarettes and a lighter.

"Did your Ma buy you this place then?"

"Aye, so what if she did?"

"And the car? The Saxo? Did she get you that an' all?"

He shrugged, "So what? She's a fuckin' millionaire, she can afford it."

"Nice pimp-job. Did you do it up yourself?"

"A mate did it. How, what's this all about?"

"Where were you between the hours of midnight and two am last Friday?"

McDuff scowled, "No idea, probably in a club, pissed, eh. How?"

132

"Which club?"

"One of the Stirling ones. I go to a few, an' I don't keep a note of what time I was in which one. Look, what's this all about? Why do you want to know where I was? I told you, I've done fuck all. This is harassment." He finally stopped handling the smokes and sparked one up.

Stark looked at McGhee and smiled. "No, Cammy, it's not harassment. Did you hear about what happened to Paul Jacobs; you know, Jonny Jacobs' nephew?"

McDuff shrugged. "Killed in a car crash. So what? I couldn't give two fucks. What's that got to do wi' me? Paper said it was an accident, eh."

"Might have been an accident or it might not. Might have been somebody ran him off the road. Can you think why anybody might want to do that, Cammy?"

"Because he was an arsehole? How would I know? I never met the boy, eh. I know his uncle was a fuckin' paedo, but. Maybe that's why?"

"Maybe it was, Cammy. Doesn't make it right though, does it? I mean, *he* wasn't a paedo an' even if his uncle was, which I don't think he was by the way, how come Paul deserved to be punished for something his uncle is supposed to have done?"

McDuff began pacing, getting to the end of his smoke, taking little care with how he disposed of the ash. "This is total bullshit, by the way. I don't know anything about Paul Jacobs or how he crashed. I've told you everything I know, so you can go now, eh."

The two detectives stood up as Stark's radio crackled into life.

"Alpha Sierra One, this is Sierra Bravo One come in, over."

"Sierra Bravo One, this is Alpha Sierra One, over."

"We have details on vehicle as requested, over."

Stark watched as McDuff lit another cigarette. "Go ahead, over."

"Citroen Saxo, Charlie Mike Delta Zero One, is

registered to Cameron McDuff of 48 Wellpark Crescent, Stirling. Tax and insurance are up to date, over."

"Ok, thanks, over."

McDuff grinned triumphantly and took a deep drag on his cigarette.

"Also, please be aware that a second vehicle is registered to this address and owner. A Range Rover, Charlie Mike Delta Zero Two. Also taxed and insured, over."

McDuff made a break for the back door but McGhee caught him before he could reach it. He grappled him to the floor, and Stark applied a set of cuffs. They hauled McDuff to his feet amid a flurry of expletives and formally arrested him for his involvement in the death of Paul Jacobs.

Cammy McDuff's new-found wealth meant he no longer had to rely on the duty solicitor. Instead, he was sitting in the interview room with Connor McKenzie, one of Alloa's finest alumni, renowned for helping the guilty get away with murder – in some cases, literally. Stark couldn't care less. He knew McDuff was involved in sending Paul Jacobs to his death and no smart-arse lawyer was going to stop him proving it.

He took his seat opposite the two men and did the formalities in terms of recording, date and time and so on. McKenzie annoyed him without even speaking. Far too well-dressed, far too clean and unblemished in that way some wealthy professionals like to assert their dominance over others with. Far too sure of himself.

"Cammy," began Stark, "why did you attempt to flee when the information about your Range Rover came through this morning?"

"No comment."

Oh great, thought Stark. This tosser of a lawyer had encouraged McDuff to stonewall him. McKenzie probably hoped their evidence was too weak to use without a confession and was probably also using it as a delaying tactic; hoping he could discover or manipulate a procedural flaw to create an escape route via a technicality. The cynic in Stark also thought it was partly to piss him off and, all the while, increase the billable hours.

"Ok, you can try the 'no comment' thing if you want but remember, it can be construed as obstructive by the court later on an' will just make this drag on longer than it has to. Of course, time is no issue to Mr McKenzie here. In fact, time is money to him. Your money."

McKenzie smiled. "Now, now detective, let's not get off on the wrong foot here. My client will comment when he feels it is appropriate to do so." He may have been from Alloa but you'd never have guessed from his accent. It had been homogenised, neutered, discarded. The type of people McKenzie associated with now would never tolerate such obvious signposts to his far humbler origins and upbringing.

"Aye, an' it's no' my money – it's my Maw's!" said McDuff, full of sneering self-satisfaction and bravado.

"So, why did you try to run away, Cammy? What are we going to find out about the Range Rover?"

"No comment."

"I suggest that we're going to find out you used it to run Paul Jacobs off the road, causing his death."

"No comment."

Stark watched McKenzie tap out a distracting tattoo with his pen on a notepad, and began to simmer.

"Where is the car, Cammy? It wasn't outside the house this morning."

McKenzie nodded.

"It's at my mate's. He's doing some custom work on it," said McDuff, barely suppressing a laugh as he said it.

"Really? I think you mean it's in for repair. Maybe getting some damage to the front sorted after its little bump the other night?"

McDuff smirked again and drew out his reply with a

flourish, "No comment!"

Stark could feel his ire increasing. Keeping cool in these situations took every bit of self-control he could rustle up. He hoped it would be enough. To react would be to let McKenzie win. He wasn't winning. No chance.

"So, who is this mate an' where's he working on the car?"

McKenzie nodded again.

"Mick Martin. He's got a wee unit at Kelliebank. Martin's Custom Cars."

"Ok, I'm going to suspend the interview for a few minutes. Please wait here," said Stark, getting up and heading into the corridor. Jim McGhee, who'd been observing through one-way glass was already waiting for him.

"I'm on it, Adam. I don't hold out much hope we'll get there in time to find the evidence intact but I'll give it a go anyway."

Stark nodded. "Right, aye, no doubt. This dickhead lawyer is just what I need by the way. How he's kept all his shiny white teeth in his mouth this long is beyond me. Smarmy bastard."

"Don't let him get to you, Adam, eh. He's dying for you to do something he can use to scupper the case. You've bought this t-shirt before. It'll be worth it to nail that little toerag McDuff. I'll see you in a bit," said McGhee, heading off to the custom car shop.

Stark returned to the interview room and recommenced the interrogation.

"We have a witness who saw your car parked outside Paul Jacobs' flat in the days leading up to his death. They said you drove off in a hurry when he ran towards you," said Stark, adding a little more certainty to this account than Mrs Campbell would be able to if she was ever called to testify.

"No comment."

"What were you doing there, Cammy? Why were you

parked in that street?"

"No comment."

"Did your dad put you up to this, Cammy? Some kind of revenge for what Jonny did, eh? Gave you the instructions during one of your visits, did he?"

"No comment."

"Ok, if you're determined to avoid answering any of my questions, I'll just call a halt to this for now. I really can't be bothered playing silly buggers with you anymore today, Cammy. We're going to get the car from that workshop an', once we've had a look over it, I'm willing to predict you'll feel the need to be a bit more helpful. In the meantime, you can go back to the cells. I'll let you know when you'll be needing Mr McKenzie's services again."

Stark switched off the recording equipment and left a constable to return McDuff to the cells. As he walked off up the corridor, McKenzie came after him.

"DI Stark, a moment, please."

He stopped and let the lawyer catch him up.

"I'd like to know how long you intend to hold my client. It seems clear to me that your evidence is flimsy and without some concrete link between the cars, you'll have nothing you can prove."

"Mr McKenzie, a young man died the other night an' we owe it to him an' his family to be as thorough as possible in pursuing whoever caused his death. I believe that person to be your client, an' I'll be holding him for as long as it takes me to prove that – within the confines of the law, obviously," replied Stark.

"Well, let's just make sure that's the case, DI Stark. Please get someone to page me when you're ready to recommence the interview."

Stark nodded and headed for his office, wishing there was a way for him to leave McKenzie spitting out those abnormally white gnashers that wouldn't see him being arrested for it. He intended to leave McDuff stewing overnight. He still had some legal leeway and he needed time to find a forensic link between the cars. He took out his phone and dialled Archie Brown. He wanted him to be ready to go as soon as McGhee found the Range Rover.

18.

Mick Martin appeared to be fond of customising his own bodywork almost as much as that of the cars he transformed from ugly ducklings into automotive swans. Although, as far as McGhee could make out, he'd got the process in reverse when it came to his personal appearance. Tattoos animated every inch of his visible skin – including his neck and shaven head – and various metallic adornments protruded from his face. He could have gotten a good price for his head at the scrapyard across the way. Nearer mute than taciturn, he was uninterested in co-operating with the cops who'd turned up to retrieve Cammy McDuff's Range Rover.

"Listen, Mick, if it turns out you've knowingly assisted an offender, this could get ugly for you. What exactly did you do to the car?" asked McGhee.

The mechanic shrugged. "Put a set of bull bars on it."

"And that was it? No damage to repair? No repainting required?"

"Naw."

McGhee could tell this guy was well-versed in sticking to a script of denial and half-truths. In his game, clients who were indulging in activities that were less than kosher or just straight-up illegal would be commonplace. This was a small, backstreet garage, not a national chain. He'd take whatever business he could in order to get by. Question-asking would be a luxury he couldn't afford. It also meant he would be well aware that some of those clients would expect him to hold his tongue if anyone in authority did come calling; in all likelihood via implied threats to his premises and person. Cammy McDuff might well be one such client, given his parentage.

"Right, well, we're going to conduct a search. Please stop whatever work you're doing, don't touch anything an' let my guys get to work."

"Fuck's sake! This is out of order. I've got a living to make here, eh."

"Aye, that's as may be, Mick, but we're investigating a suspicious death an' you'd better hope you've no' got yourself involved in it 'cause, last time I checked, there wasn't a lot of demand for customising cars inside Glenochil Prison."

The mechanic stomped off, lighting a smoke as he went, and sat down in a plastic chair outside the work unit. Perched there with a face like thunder and his arms crossed over his chest, Mick Martin looked like someone you wouldn't mess with. McGhee could imagine many a person would cross the street to avoid him, even if he maybe wasn't as fierce as his external appearance might suggest. Of course, McGhee knew nothing about the guy, so it could well be that avoidance was indeed the sensible option. The extensive ink, shaven head, trunk-like limbs and facial metalwork were deliberate statements, with a clear intention to create an aura of menace – deserved or not.

McGhee and one of the two constables he'd brought with him began their search. The other junior officer kept watch over the sulking proprietor.

The workshop met all of McGhee's preconceived notions – cluttered, dirty, reeking of chemicals and paint, and cramped. It didn't take long to find nothing of note. There was no time to trawl through the various scattered piles of paperwork, so the constable gathered, bagged and tagged them and stuck them in the boot of a squad car. They could be sifted later, back at the station. As the cops gathered again at the front of the unit, Archie Brown pulled up. After a brief exchange with McGhee, he and another technician got on with checking over the Range Rover. Mick Martin sat in his chair, looking on, smoking and fuming.

McGhee and the two constables began a sweep of the environs of the unit. McGhee walked around to the back of the garage. It was rough ground, unkempt and litter-strewn. His attention was drawn to a dark-coloured tarpaulin against the back wall of the units. The most interesting thing about it was how dry it appeared, despite the overnight rain only abating an hour or so before they arrived at Martin's Custom Cars. He walked over to it and put on a pair of latex gloves. Pulling at the waxy sheet of material revealed an object underneath. A set of black bull bars, dented and marked with a few flecks of yellow paint. It looked like Mick Martin didn't get any warning from Cammy McDuff about McGhee's impending visit. McDuff probably assumed the mechanic would already have removed the evidence and didn't feel it necessary to get a message to him. Luckily for McGhee and the rest of the team, it turned out Martin had delayed the more thorough disposal McDuff would have expected. He radioed Archie Brown and phoned Stark to let him know the good news.

The meeting Stark and McGhee had with DCI McLaren was brief. The case was done. Paul Jacobs killed the Cook girl – probably as a result of being rejected sexually, although that was nothing more than conjecture given neither of the main parties involved were able to corroborate it – and Cammy McDuff killed Jacobs in revenge for his uncle's kidnapping escapades. Despite the uncovering of such damning evidence, McDuff maintained his rigid, two word answering regime as his weasel lawyer tried to claim all sorts of mitigating circumstances and justifications on his behalf. Stark could accept that McDuff never set out to murder Jacobs. However, it was obvious the boy hadn't properly considered the potential consequences his preferred method of punishment might have. He also didn't do himself any favours by trying, and failing, to cover up the evidence from the collision. If the weasel was as good as people claimed he was, then McDuff might only end up facing a lesser charge of culpable homicide. Either way, he'd be following in his father's dubious, incarcerated footsteps.

As far as the Police Scotland senior brass were concerned, it was a good result. Backs would be getting slapped, the public would sleep easy knowing the bogey man had been vanquished, and the circumstances meant they'd save a fortune by avoiding Debbie Cook's case going to court. McLaren could barely disguise his glee once they'd talked it all through. Somehow, though, Stark couldn't share his boss's delight. So many questions remained, so many issues would raise their heads as a result.

If he was Paul Jacobs' parent, he'd be shattered to have his murdered son go to his grave being denounced as a murderer himself; a fiend who forced a beautiful young woman into a river and then plagued her cousin (who was supposed to be his best friend) with cruel taunts afterwards. It might well be scant, and remain unproven in a court of law, but the evidence strongly suggested it was so. Not only that but the media were about to compound the Jacobs' misery many times over due to the minor celebrity status of their son. The salacious and juicy details of the McDuff kidnapping would be wheeled out again; made all the more poignant and newsworthy by Uncle Jonny's sudden demise. Endless pages would be devoted to cod-psychology and hand-wringing about how it all went wrong. Speculation and insinuation would become an art form. Stark particularly baulked at the hackneyed bleating from the press about 'what lessons could be learnt to stop this happening again'. There are six billion people on this planet, all with a myriad of individual drives, mental constitutions and moral frameworks. Imagining there was some way to legislate for every eventuality was, and is, a pointless exercise. Take aeroplanes, for example. They make the cockpit impregnable to terrorists, thus preventing hijack or deliberate crashing, and the unwitting consequence is it helps a suicidal pilot commit his own kind of atrocity. Until it happened, who could have predicted such a thing? As far as Stark could see, the best folk could do was carry on, brace themselves for the next time and just hope, whatever it was, it didn't happen to them.

If he was Grant or Anne Cook, he'd be devastated to know his only daughter had been killed by a close family friend, a boy he'd known for so many years.

If he was Colin Cook, he'd be inconsolable and bewildered as to why a person he regarded as his best friend would have done this to him and his family. This sadistic edge to it still puzzled Stark. What had Colin Cook done to deserve such cruelty from a lifelong friend?

The whys would be a torture for all of them. Made many times worse by having no-one left standing to provide answers. Stark, at least, would soon find himself distracted by other matters and his torment would only surface on rare occasions. For the others, it would be constant and all-consuming.

Ian Barr was glad they'd settled the Cook case. He wasn't glad the Cooks' and Jacobs' lives had been put through a blender but he would be relieved to get back to dealing with burglaries, fraud and car-ringing. Unlike some of his more ambitious colleagues, Barr had begun to realise he neither enjoyed nor wanted the responsibility of dealing with murders and rapes and such like. Maybe becoming a father had softened him. If it had, it was a trade he didn't regret.

It was the end of the shift and time to get home to his family. As he walked past reception, Jane called him over.

"Ian, some guy just phoned in. Says he saw the sign on the road asking for information regarding the Paul Jacobs' accident."

"Oh, right. We've pretty much sorted that out now,

Jane. I'll get someone to go and collect that sign tomorrow. What was he saying, anyway?"

"Something about seeing a car parked at the side of the road there that night with its hazard lights on. Had to swerve to avoid it."

Barr nodded. "Range Rover, black, private number plate? Aye, we know about it but thanks anyway, Jane. See you later."

The receptionist's brow creased and she looked over the top of her glasses at Barr. "Actually, Ian, that's not his description of the car at all."

Barr, who'd begun to walk away, stopped and turned back. "Really? That's funny. Have you got the guy's details?"

"Yes, here you go," she said handing him a slip of paper.

"Thanks, Jane. See you tomorrow."

Barr walked to his car and took the slip of paper from his pocket. This was a bit odd, but likely irrelevant. They had clear forensic evidence that Cammy McDuff's car had been used to push Jacobs off the road. Either the witness was mixing up the nights or it was a strange coincidence. He couldn't think why someone other than McDuff would have stopped, seen the car in the ditch, and not tried to help or call the emergency services. Whatever the case, he was tired and needed to get home to Kirsty and the nipper. She was heavily pregnant again and would be exhausted by now. He'd go home, make the tea and give the wee one a bath. Sometimes work wasn't the most important thing in life to a copper.

***

Stark closed up the laptop and took the glass of whisky over to the couch with him. He switched on the television and slumped back in the chair. The usual guff prevailed. There was some football on in a bit, so he would bide his time until then, channel-hopping.

The card was like one of those paintings where the eyes follow you around the room. It lay on the coffee table, imploring him to act. His long-running excuse of being embroiled in a difficult case no longer applied, so why couldn't he bring himself to call her? All his life Stark had been successful with women; a string of short-term and slightly longer relationships lay behind him. He liked the company of women. He liked having someone to share things with, to argue with, to joke around with, to spoil, to rely on, to desire and to be wanted by. But as each person he thought might be the one to stick the course bailed on him, a chip of confidence came loose and fell away. This had mostly gone unnoticed by Stark, the process so gradual and each step so seemingly insignificant that he failed to spot the cumulative effect. He didn't want to admit it, but the rejection in the pub those few weeks ago was a real blow to his sense of self; the first chip to come away from the foundations. It had left his ego wobbling like a tower block in an earthquake. He worried that Madeline could cause the kind of aftershock that might tip it over.

The whisky glinted as some film or other filled the otherwise unlit room with artificial sunshine. He stared at the liquid and thought about how easily he'd stopped drinking in the past. All this wallowing and tedious self-analysis had only crept up on him since he began indulging again. He'd been snared by the illusion that drink offered solace, comfort and relaxation when, in fact, it sought out your misery, your insecurity and your doubts and brought them barging to the front of your mind – convincing you that you needed more alcohol to force them back. A duplicitous, sneaky bastard, that's what whisky was. He sat forward, took the cap off the bottle and poured back the remains of his glass, picked up the phone, slid the card toward him and dialled.

19.

Colin ran like he'd not run in an age. Like he used to when the glory of representing his country beckoned. The machine hummed as his feet slapped down. Since discovering music helped him run better, he'd taken to always filling his head with tunes that maintained tempo and momentum, songs that spurred him on when the pain tried to tear chunks out of his resolve. But it wasn't the playlist that drove him to excel today. It was rage.

The police sat them all down and talked through their theories, presented their case, explained what had happened – as far as they could deduce, given the obvious gaps in their knowledge and evidence. Expletives and angry outbursts rattled around the room. Denials, disgust, outrage and fury were followed by tears and bitter silence. His aunt left the room avoiding his gaze and refusing to speak to him. She didn't come right out with it, but Colin could tell she thought he was partly to blame for bringing Paul Jacobs into their lives and that, as his friend, he should have known something, done something. Worst of all, he suspected she even thought he might be involved somehow.

He thought about Paul, about what he was supposed to have done. It wouldn't compute; he couldn't believe it. For all the public brashness and bravado, Colin knew a different Paul. That Paul would never have killed Debbie. That Paul would never have sent those texts. The police were wrong, he was sure of it but, like them, he couldn't come up with a better answer.

The gym was quiet. He didn't usually come here but he'd decided to avoid running on the road until he was sure his ankle was going to hold up. He could also go for a swim if he fancied it. The only other patrons were a preening body-builder, who spent all his time admiring his fake-tanned physique in a mirror while doing weights, and a middle-aged woman who huffed and puffed on a rowing machine across the way from him. The exposed parts of her skin glistened with sweat and her face glowed with the scarlet of proper exertion. Years of neglect probably being tackled a little too late. Still, fair play to her. At least she was giving it a go – no matter how tardy or futile her efforts might prove to be.

When the fire alarm went off, he assumed it was a test, until one of the staff informed him otherwise. No need to panic, make his way outside, don't stop to retrieve his property, blah, blah, blah. It was just his luck that a false alarm would happen on the morning he was about to smash his personal best. As he stood in the car park waiting to be allowed back in, slowly chilling down, his thoughts turned back to recent events and his mood darkened further. Part of him hoped the fucking place would burn to the ground.

"Excuse me, do you want to sit in the car and keep warm while they're sorting all of this out?"

He'd been snapped out of his black reverie by the puce-faced woman from the rowing machine. As she smiled sweetly, Colin decided she was actually very attractive, for her age. Another gust of wind rippled through his flimsy vest and shorts, helping him to make up his mind. He shrugged, made his way over to the car and got in the passenger seat of the silver VW Golf she was driving.

"Thanks. It's all a bit of a pain in the backside this, isn't it?" he said.

"Yes, it's the fact you have to come down here in a state of half undress. It's Scotland, for goodness' sake. Luckily, I had my car keys with me. I don't like leaving them in a locker."

"Aye, well, thanks for the shelter. That wind is pretty nippy when you've got next to bugger-all on."

148

Colin began to feel a little awkward. After he'd sat down and closed the door, he realised she was indeed in a state of half undress – a crop-top, lycra training vest that exposed her arms and midriff and had a plunging neckline. He struggled to keep his eyes off her ample cleavage and, close up, he found her even more alluring than from across the car park. Her long, curly, blonde hair framed an oval face, pronounced cheekbones and sparkling blue eyes. At close quarters, her lycra shorts revealed her bare legs to be longer and leaner than he'd thought they were while she'd been working out. There was something vaguely familiar about her but he couldn't place her. Probably a likeness to some pop singer or actress that made him think he knew her when, in fact, he didn't. Whether he'd ever met her before or not, it had been a long time since he'd been in close proximity to such an attractive, semi-clad female; he could feel stirrings down below that he hoped he'd be able to control. With only his shorts on, there would be no hiding place for his arousal.

"My name's Sara," she said extending her hand.

"Colin."

They shook hands. Colin felt the heat rise in his face and his groin as she held on a little longer than he'd expected, maintaining eye contact. Her eyes were amazing, almost *too* blue. Something flashed in them. It was fleeting but just for a second he thought he sensed something. Then she smiled, revealing a set of perfect white teeth and the sensation melted away. The weird thing was this woman may well have been ages with his mother, but he didn't care. She was gorgeous and he was pretty sure she was flirting with him now.

"Nice to meet you, Colin."

Her voice was refined; Scottish but posh Scottish, rather than the local dialect. Sexy. She released her grip and reached over into the back seat of the car. Her hair brushed against him and the smell of exercise mixed with her perfume and hairspray wafted into his nostrils. He squirmed as an erection began to take shape. She sat back around and held up a flask.

"Would you like a wee cup of coffee? Help warm you up."

Glad of the distraction, Colin nodded and thanked her. He took the small cup that was part of the lid and took a sip. His hands were trembling but it wasn't the cold causing it.

"Sorry, are you not having any?" he asked, offering the cup back to her.

"No, I'm fine. I had a wee drop before. You carry on – you look like you need it," she said, the smile beaming. "There's only that one cup anyway."

The warmth from the coffee was welcome and he felt himself unwinding. Colin looked out of the window, trying not to give his expanding member any further encouragement. He sniggered as daft images formed in his head – his erect penis, spray-tanned, lifting weights and admiring itself in mirror. A proud member of the gym. Just like that bell-end of a body builder.

"What's so funny?"

"Oh, nothing, just thinking about something a friend said. Not funny to anyone else, really. Sorry."

She smiled again but it was awkward, puzzled. A silence descended on the two of them and he tried not to look at her chest or her legs. He drained the first cup and, without being asked, Sara refilled his cup.

Outside, the gym was returning to normal. The shrieking alarm had been silenced and it looked as if the milling, restless knots of customers and staff were being allowed back in. There were a lot more folk than Colin expected, given how low the gym attendance had been.

Colin felt so comfortable in the warm car, with this beautiful woman by his side. He didn't really want to go back inside. Sara made no suggestion that they should do so and they sat there, not talking, just relaxing, enjoying the peace. It was hypnotic and he felt all the turmoil of the past few hours subsiding. He looked over at Sara and his eyelids drooped. He shook his head as a crushing weariness swept over him. There was that dazzling smile again, those legs, that hair, those breasts. He nodded again. The empty cup dropped into his lap as he drifted away into the calm black.

***

The Italian restaurant was Madeline's idea. The call had been a little awkward, his apologies for taking so long to contact her profuse and sincere. She took a bit of convincing that he could, or even should, make it up to her but he managed it in the end.

It was a lunchtime date as opposed to an evening one. Stark guessed this was partly to avoid giving him any hope that something more might follow on after eating. As they were both working straight afterwards, it also removed alcohol from the equation. A sober, informal, strictly time-bound first date. Not what he'd have chosen but if he'd just had the bottle to phone her when he said he would, it might have been very different. Regardless of the mechanics of venue or timing, he was still crapping himself. She was five minutes late and his nerves were shredded. Was she going to stand him up in retaliation for his nonchalant approach to asking her out?

The door opened and Madeline came in out of the rain, folding her brolly and allowing the waiter to take her rain coat to hang up. She smiled and waved before making her way over to the table. He stood and she pecked him on the cheek. The touch of her skin had its usual effect on him.

"Hi, sorry I'm a bit late," she said, grabbing a menu.

"No bother, it's only a couple of minutes. Nice weather again. Lucky you don't have too far to walk."

She looked up and smiled. A tingle wound its way up his spine.

"You been here before then?" asked Stark.

151

"A few times. It's good and as you've pointed out, it's handy for work lunches and stuff."

"Is that what this is then? Work?" said Stark, winking.

"Oh, no, this is far less enjoyable than that!"

They both laughed as the waiter approached to take their orders.

As Stark sat in his car watching Madeline scurry into the bank through the sheeting rain, he could feel an optimism rising in him that had been absent for some time. Conversation had been easy and candid. They both liked sports, but most surprising was Madeline's love of hard rock music. They had a couple of mutual acquaintances and they'd both suffered loss. Madeline was almost as alone in the world as he was. She still had her big sister around but her mother passed away a few years back. Her father left when she was small and died before she ever got a chance to reconcile with him. She'd told Stark about her ex-husband who'd run off with a girl he worked with, got her pregnant, then left her as well. A right charmer. It helped make her resilient, self-reliant, and probably more wary of commitment than was healthy. He knew how that felt. They'd agreed to meet again and he was already looking forward to it.

He picked up his mobile and looked at the display. A text message from Ian Barr had arrived while he'd been eating. It said it was urgent that Stark get back to the station as soon as he could. He put the car into gear and drove off.

20.

Duncan Cook was pacing back and forth across the reception area as Stark walked into the station. When he saw Stark, he almost bundled into him in a frantic attempt to stop him passing by.

"Detective Stark, you need to get out there an' find my boy before something terrible happens to him!"

All of Cook's vital signs appeared to be red-lining. Stark assumed this was the urgent thing Ian Barr was referring to, but he was unsettled by this demand without any context to put it into.

"Ok, Mr Cook, I'm sorry but I've not been at work this morning. I don't know what you're talking about. Has something happened to Colin?"

"Of course something's happened to Colin. You need to get your act together an' go an' find him!" Cook bellowed.

Stark tried to regain some personal space as Ian Barr appeared.

"Mr Cook. I really have no idea at all what you're talking about. Can we take this into a more private area where you can update me an' I can try to help?"

"Hi, sir. Sorry, I was just coming down to take Mr Cook to an interview room," said Barr. "Can you follow me please, Mr Cook?" He gestured toward the open door leading through into the main part of the building.

Once in the room, Cook refused to sit; restless, fidgeting, borderline manic. Stark sat down and took out his notebook.

"Right, Mr Cook. Can you start at the beginning, please; what's going on?"

"Colin's gone missing, I already told you that, eh. I want you to find him an' bring him back home."

"Can you be a bit more specific, please, Mr Cook? How an' when did this happen?"

"He went to the gym early this morning an' he's no' come home, eh. He's no' answering his phone an' when I went down to the gym, they said he left hours ago, after a fire alarm went off."

Stark looked at Barr, who shrugged.

"What?" asked Cook, getting animated again. "It's not right. He wouldn't just disappear like that. Not after all that's happened recently. Something bad has happened, I just know it has." Cook finally stopped moving about the room and sat down with a thump in one of the chairs, his breathing heavy and erratic. He loosened his tie and took a sip of water. Stark was concerned the businessman might collapse at any moment.

"Mr Cook, I know this is hard. You've been through a hell of a lot in the past few weeks. I understand why you're concerned an' are thinking the worst but you need to calm down. Colin is a grown man. He's only been gone a few hours. The phone might be out of charge or he might be somewhere like a cinema wi' it switched off. There are hundreds of possible reasons why he might …"

"You don't get it, do you? This isn't normal. He's been under a huge amount of stress since Debbie was killed by that scumbag Paul Jacobs. He's not himself. I'm really worried it's all got too much for him an' he's going to do something stupid."

Stark let him calm down a bit before continuing.

"Alright, Mr Cook. I normally wouldn't do this but given everything that's gone on before, I'll speak to the gym to get some more specific timings, an' I'll put out an alert to all our guys to look out for him. That's the best I can do for now. Have you tried phoning his friends, relatives further afield he might have decided to visit on a whim, that sort of thing?"

"No' really. I suppose I should do that. I'll go back to the office an' make some calls. Let me know as soon as you hear anything."

"I will do, sir. Try not to worry. I'm sure this is all perfectly innocent an' he'll be back soon enough. If you find him before we do, please let me know. Thanks for coming in. I'll be in touch," said Stark.

Cook got up and Barr led him back out to reception.

Stark sat back in the chair, clasped his hands behind his head and let out a long sigh. He could understand the man's concern but they'd made a rod for their backs trying to stay on the good side of these supposed local dignitaries. The laddie probably just needed a break from his father. He was one intense guy.

Barr came back into the room. "Sorry, sir. I got delayed going to get him. If I'd known you were so close by, I'd have given you more warning."

"Ach, don't worry about it Ian. He's just being over-protective, which is totally understandable in the circumstances. It's bound to be nothing but do me a favour an' check out the gym for me. Ask them when he got there, when he left, see if they've got any CCTV."

"Ok, sir. I'll let you know what they say," said Barr making for the door before stopping and turning back to face Stark.

"Oh, by the way, I meant to say to you: we had someone come forward in relation to the Jacobs' crash. I thought they were going to confirm seeing McDuff's Range Rover but they didn't. I know that case is supposed to be boxed off but it seemed a bit odd. I spoke to the guy this morning out of curiosity an' he was adamant that on the night of the crash he had to swerve around a silver VW Golf that was parked just past that bend with its hazards on."

Stark frowned. "Really? Why was somebody parked there? Not the handiest place to stop for a piss."

"That's what I thought, sir. The guy says he only just

155

managed to avoid it."

"An' what time was this?"

"About one-thirty. He said he knows that because he'd been at a friend's twenty-first birthday party that finished about one, an' he was on his way home, eh."

Stark stood up, indicating that they should walk and talk. "That's right in the window of when Jacobs died according to the post-mortem. If they stopped there, why didn't they help or report it?"

"I know, again, I had the same thought, sir. What were they doing?"

"Did the guy get a registration?"

"No, he says it happened too quick. To be fair, at least he managed make an' model. We could have had silver car or even just car, eh," said Barr, chuckling.

"Ah, well. I don't think it's worth wasting too much time on. We know McDuff caused the crash an', as far as we can tell, the Jacobs laddie was just unlucky that ditch was full of water combined wi'' getting trapped by his leg. All I can think of is that the guy reporting this has got something wrong in relation to timing or even location. It might have been a different bend?"

"Aye, maybe, sir, but he seemed pretty on the ball to me. Anyway, just thought I'd better keep you up to speed, eh. I'll go an' speak to these gym folk now."

"Alright, Ian. No worries, I'll catch up wi' you in a bit."

Stark sat down at his desk and his thoughts drifted back to Madeline. He needed to take the initiative, be bold, arrange the next date. He opened up his email and knocked out a quick message asking if she'd like to go to see a film or have a meal that weekend. He hit send and got back to his paperwork. The court date for the fraud case he'd been working before all this Cook business started up was looming. Those kind of cases needed meticulous planning to avoid the fraudster finding a legal bolthole to use. But he was distracted and unfocused while he waited for her reply. The complexities and nuance of the case were sailing past, adrift on his sea of euphoria. If he didn't think so before, he now knew he had it bad.

***

Colin felt cold … and wet, which was odd. Shivers wracked through him as he came back to consciousness. His thoughts felt dulled and jumbled. He struggled to think what might be going on. Snippets of information floated in and out of reach. A car, a woman, the gym, a fire.

Why was he wet?

His eyes wouldn't focus when they opened and he realised he wasn't wearing his glasses. He was in a bath. Naked and lying in a bath. How the hell had that happened? The water only lapped against his sides and the back of his head, barely a couple of inches deep. That's why he was so cold. Colin tried to move his hands towards his face, to rub his cloudy eyes and they wouldn't shift. They were tied together above his head. His legs were bound as well. Fear surged through him and he thrashed about, causing the ropes to dig into his flesh. He began to shout and that's when he noticed the tape over his mouth. The fear turned to panic.

After a few minutes of pointless and increasingly painful flailing, he stopped and tried to get to grips with what was going on. His thoughts were still opaque – like a lace curtain had been pulled over his mind; not entirely blotting out the light but doing enough to preserve privacy, obscure the view. He could remember being at the gym, running like the wind. The woman in the car. The beautiful blonde. The warmth, the coffee, relaxing. Now this. This insanity.

Colin looked around but his vantage point was limited by the sides of the bath and his defective eyesight. A tiled wall, the ropes attached to moorings at either end of the bath – moorings that looked nothing like the standard fittings most bathrooms had. As if they were bespoke for the purpose. The taps down at the end where his feet were. A light-fitting in a featureless ceiling was the only other landmark he could discern.

This was a big bath. Colin was over six foot tall and yet he was lying flat out with room to spare. The sides of the bath seemed uncommonly tall as well, which in part explained why he could see so little. What was this? Why had someone tied him up in a bath? Was it some kind of sick, sexual fantasy – had she been reading too many of those shitty erotic novels that had become so trendy and popular amongst women of her age lately? If it wasn't that, if it wasn't pleasure masquerading as pain, then what? What had he done to cause this? But he knew the answer to that. In a blinding moment of realisation, the lace curtain was pulled clear from his mind as he remembered who she was. She looked more glamorous, the hair was different, she'd dropped the big specs, but it was definitely her. That had to be why he was here and now he wasn't just scared, he was terrified.

The door opened and closed out of view and he began to thrash about again as she appeared above him, looking down, the blonde wig gone, the contact lenses removed, less revealing clothing, the glasses back on.

"Hello, Coco. I bet you remember me, now, don't you?"

He did and he was sorry.

So very sorry.

21.

The leisure centre manager looked ill at ease. One of those people who inexplicably felt a sense of foreboding in the presence of an officer of the law; even though she'd done nothing wrong personally, she assumed she was the one about to get into serious bother.

"This is probably nothing, Janet," said Ian Barr, "but we're just checking it out to reassure a concerned parent, eh."

Janet Gibson nodded and fidgeted with a pen lying on her desk, avoiding eye contact. "We had a false alarm this morning. Someone broke a panel. We thought it might be a kid messing about but when we checked the CCTV we were surprised to see it was an adult. They were walking down the corridor, stumbled and knocked against it."

"And they didn't come an' apologise or admit what they'd done?"

"No, not as far as I know. We did the evacuation, as per our manual, reset the system, then let everyone back in again. It was inconvenient but not the crime of the century, you know."

Barr acknowledged this and checked his notes. "Did you take a register of any kind? I mean, do you have a record of everyone who was in the building at the time that you cross-reference to make sure they're all out safe?"

Janet looked startled, like he was putting her on trial as far as her health and safety procedures were concerned. "Em, not really. We do a sweep of the building to check no-one has been left inside but we don't call a register or anything like that. I mean, some folk would just have left straight away. It's not like we can insist they stay put."

"No, no, that's ok, Janet. I just wondered, eh. Do you

know who came in that morning, though? Do folk need to sign in at the desk, show a membership card, that sort of thing?"

"Yes, they do. I can tell you if someone was here before and after the alarm," she said, the gleam of sweat on her brow being highlighted by the fluorescent light above her.

"Great. Can you check if a Colin Cook was here before an' after the alarm, please?"

Janet called the desk and after a brief exchange was able to confirm that Colin Cook had been in before the alarm but had not returned afterwards. She also confirmed that Duncan Cook had been in to enquire about his son earlier in the afternoon.

"Do you know if he used a locker for his things?" asked Barr.

"I'm not sure. He probably would have, I suppose. Most people do."

"Do you mind if we go an' have a wee look; check if he left his things behind or took them wi' him?"

Janet got up from her desk and gestured for them to leave the room. "Ok, let's go up to the changing rooms."

The lockers were operated using a pound coin, returned to the user when they replaced the key in the lock to re-open the door and retrieve their valuables or clothing. Unused lockers had the key in the lock attached to a green, rubberised wrist-strap with a number on it corresponding to the one on the locker door. There were ten lockers in use at that point with another forty or so not. Barr quickly looked through all the open ones, just in case, but the most he found were a couple of sweet wrappers, a pen, an odd sock and a pair of damp swimming trunks. Certainly, nothing of note that might belong to Colin Cook.

"Is there any way to tell which lockers are being used by the folks on site at the moment?" he asked Janet.

"Apart from approaching the customers and asking

them? No. It's not computerised or anything like that."

Janet was finding her feet, beginning to relax, feeling less paranoid.

"Can I do that, then? Go an' ask folk what locker they're using?"

"Err, I suppose so, yes."

It took Barr about fifteen minutes to track down nine of the ten keys. The remaining locker was number twelve.

"Do you have a master key for these lockers, Janet?"

"Yes, I have one here," she replied, taking a keyring with several keys on it from her pocket. She opened the locker and stood back. Inside was a pile of clothing, a watch and a mobile phone. Barr donned a pair of gloves and took the phone out, pressing the start button as he did so. The home screen came to life, showing a photo of Debbie and Colin Cook as young kids. A photo he'd seen while examining Debbie Cook's laptop. His concern for Colin Cook's safety began to increase. Why would the boy have walked away and left his clothes, phone and watch behind? He put the phone back in the locker and asked Janet to lock it up again.

"Janet. Can you make sure no-one else goes near that locker for now, please?"

"Yes, ok. I'll ask one of the girls to come up and keep an eye on it." Her nervousness returned with gusto as she radioed for a member of her team to come up and babysit the locker.

"Thanks, Janet. Listen, does your CCTV cover the car park or the outside of the building?"

"It does, yes. It's not brilliant outside but there are cameras on the doors, which should show everyone coming in and out."

"Great, can we take a look at that, please?"

"Yes, if you follow me, I'll take you to the control room."

They were able to concentrate on the time around the

alarm being triggered and it didn't take too long for them to spot Colin Cook leaving the building. He was wearing running gear, no watch on his wrist and no bag with him. Barr asked them to switch to the outside view. Cook hung about the front of the building for a couple of minutes, avoiding the other people doing likewise, then appeared to make his way into the car park and get into the passenger seat of a silver VW Golf. Barr felt the hairs on his neck rise. A silver Golf – the same make and model as the guy reported being parked hazardously near Jacobs' crash site. It could be nothing to do with the car Cook got into but his instincts were tingling.

"Can we zoom in an' get a better look at that registration number?" asked Barr.

"Not right now, I'm afraid," said the technician operating the equipment, "if the picture was live I could but this is a recording. You'd need to take it away and digitally manipulate it on a computer."

"Right, can you make me a hard copy of that file or send me it as a link to my email?"

"Aye, no probs, I'll burn it onto a CD for you."

They watched the footage for a while and as everyone else returned to the building, the silver Golf drove off. As far as Barr could tell, with Colin Cook still in it.

Barr thanked Janet Gibson for all her help and made his way outside to think and call Stark for some advice.

He laid out what he'd found out so far to his boss. Stark listened in fascination. This was a very strange development. He had a strong suspicion that he'd been right not to gloat along with his bosses about boxing all this off, but he remained cautious about jumping to conclusions.

"This is all a bit weird, Ian. See if you can get the registration on that car an' follow it up wi' the owner. There are a few options. This is a gym. It's populated by fit young things, so it might be our boy got lucky an' is, as we speak, indulging in some kind of horizontal workout."

"Ha ha, aye, good one, sir. I never even thought of that, eh."

"Yeah, but there are more sinister possibilities, Ian. The silver Golf thing is making me nervous. Given what's gone on before wi' this family, I'll be happier once we've tracked the laddie down an' made sure he's ok."

"Aye, it's the car that's bothering me too, sir. I don't like those kind of coincidences, eh. I'll get on wi' finding the owner an' I'll let you know how I get on."

"Nice one, Ian. Well done. I'll see you in a bit; hopefully, wi' good news relating to our boy's sexual prowess, as opposed to something else."

"Oh, what about the locker, sir? I got one of the staff to watch it for now, in case Cook or someone else came back to it. Will I ask them to keep an eye out until closing time an' if we think anything untoward has happened, we can come back tomorrow an' get forensics onto it?"

"That's a good shout, Ian. Cheers."

"Cheers, sir."

Barr took the CD into Calum Murphy who soon resolved the image to the point where he could make out the plate. A quick check on the ANPR system and he had a name and address. He called Stark as requested.

"Hi, sir. I've got a name and address for the Golf driver. Sara Glass, lives on the edge of the Ochils in Alva. I'm just about to go an' speak to her now."

"Righto, Ian. Good stuff. Let me know as soon as you find out anything of note. Cheers."

"Will do, sir. Cheers."

***

Colin trembled with the combined effects of shock and cold. Sara Glass, the mother of Davey Glass, sat on the side of the bath and looked him up and down. All the pretence and subterfuge from the car earlier in the day was gone. Pure, unadulterated hatred burned in her eyes – back to their natural, dark brown again without their temporary blue disguise. Her voice, back to it's normal, local accent crackled with venom and Colin knew why. He'd always known this day would come. The reckoning.

"Poor little Coco. Are you scared?" She reached down and splashed the water at his side. "Ooh, that's a bit cold, eh. We'll see if we can sort that out in a minute."

Tears began to leak down his temples and snot formed in his nostrils as he fought for control.

"Ah, there, there Coco. It'll soon be over. I've been watching you for a while, you ken. How's that ankle by the way?"

Colin thought back to the silent driver who caused him to fall. It had been her. Why hadn't she sorted him out then? What was the point of waiting to get him here? If she wanted revenge, why didn't she just properly run him over?

"I know, you'll be wondering why I didn't just use the car to kill you but, to be honest, Coco, that would've been far too easy on you. You deserve to suffer, to know what it's like to be powerless, to be bullied and pushed about by someone much stronger than you. To be so desperate but to feel like no one can help you. Like my beautiful wee boy did, at the hands of you three monsters, eh."

The tone of her voice was so much more chilling than the frigid liquid lapping against him in the bath. She wasn't shouting or emotional. Just hard, bitter and determined.

She stood up, moved to the end of the bath and turned on the taps. She let the water flow gently, rather than gush forth, prolonging the moment, increasing his torment. The hot water scalded his right foot and leg as it reached them. At the same time the cold hit his left side. He yelped in surprise and pain, throwing his legs upwards out of the water, his fear now far beyond any hope of him controlling it.

"Do you know why I've put you in here, Coco?"

He tried to let her know that he did but was thrashing again, trying to escape the worst effects of the hot water as it progressed down the bath and reached parts he was finding it much harder to keep clear of the surface than his legs. He was determined to test the moorings and ropes to their maximum.

She turned off the taps as the water was close to covering his stomach. "He went for a bath wi' a bottle of pills an' drowned. But you knew that, didn't you? An', you know what, even though you weren't there, you might as well have been holding his head under."

Colin was shouting apologies, pleading with her and, although the tape did a pretty good job of muffling the words, she knew what he was saying. She didn't care. The look in her eyes was like nothing Colin had ever seen another human being direct towards him.

"I bet you're sorry now, Coco. Now I've got you tied up in a bath an' you're shitting yourself. Where was your apology after he died? What happened to your admission of guilt back then? Just like Debbie, you sat back an' let him do it. That piece of shit Jacobs made Davey's life a misery an' you did nothing, you let him, you encouraged him. An' when Davey died, you closed ranks, pretended you had nothing to do wi' it; got on wi' your lives. The little rich kids, the superstar football player, the artist, an' the athlete. Bastards! You killed him. My beautiful boy."

She moved back to the taps and turned the water back on. Again, although the flow was slow, the hot water caused him to start thrashing about but the bonds and the fixtures used to attach them were too strong. Blood was streaming from his wrists and ankles where the ropes cut deep into his flesh.

Colin watched as she stood over the bath with tears running down her cheeks looking upwards. "Well, Davey, my darling boy. We're nearly there, son. He's the last of them. I told you I'd get them for you an' I have."

She looked down at Colin and he could feel the water rising up the side of his face. He thought about Debbie and Paul, about his mum and dad, all the things he would never know. His apologies were no use to Sara Glass, she was clearly insane. The fight ebbed out of him and he lay still, waiting for the water to come and take him away just like it had taken Debbie, Paul and poor wee Davey Glass.

Davey Glass with the enormous ass. Fat-ass-Glass. Fat loser, fat bastard, fat fuck. Fat, fat, fatty. He thought about the taunting; the scale of it. Colin couldn't remember when it started but it was Paul that instigated it. For some reason, Davey Glass came in for a power of abuse, and Colin and Debbie stood by and watched or, worse still, joined in. He relived that last fateful day.

Paul tripped Davey Glass, causing him to drop a chocolate bar he was eating. Paul ground it into the dirt under his heel and laughed as the boy burst into tears. Debbie and Colin laughed along with him.

"Leave me alone!" pleaded Davey.

"Fuck off, Fat Boy Not Slim! I'm doing you a favour. You need a lot less of those fucking things, as far as I can see," was Paul's response.

"I can't take any more of this, if you don't leave me alone, I'm going to kill myself."

In hindsight, there was a look in the boy's eyes, a resignation. He was broken and Paul, Colin and Debbie were the ones who'd inflicted the damage. It didn't matter that it was Paul who was the ring leader. Colin and Debbie were willing accomplices. They didn't stick the knife in but they certainly helped to twist it.

And then, those words came from Paul's lips that couldn't be retracted, that couldn't be changed. "Go on then, do it, fat-ass. See if we care. See if anyone cares. Even your Mum will be glad to see the back of you. Save her a fucking fortune in pies!"

Davey Glass said nothing. He got back to his feet and

walked off sobbing, and that's when Colin and Debbie sank to their lowest point. Amid raucous laughter, they agreed with Paul. They confirmed his assertions. They helped Davey Glass make up his mind.

She reached down and took off the tape but he couldn't speak at first, he just looked at her. After a few seconds, he asked her the questions he now knew the answers to.

"Did you kill Debbie?"

"I didn't kill her, Coco. I just gave her a little something to ease her on her way, an' persuaded her that it was better for all of us if she jumped. And, luckily, she agreed."

Colin stifled a sob and she just smiled at him. "And Paul? Do you want to know if I killed him too?"

He nodded.

"Yes, I helped that evil piece of shit on his way. I got lucky there as well. I had planned on using the bath on him as well but, when he ended up in that ditch, it was too good an opportunity to pass up. He begged me to help him but I couldn't even speak to him. I just stopped him getting a hold of the car and let the water do the rest. I made him feel how Davey must have felt. I made him pay."

"It was you sending the texts."

"Yes, it was. I took his keys an' planted the phone in PJ's flat after the crash. A nice touch I thought. Didn't you?"

Again, Colin sobbed. This time it came out more like a wail.

She just smiled that joyless smile again.

Colin squirmed as the water got into his ear and his thoughts returned to his friend, his family and Davey. Poor wee Davey Glass.

He was so sorry.

So very sorry.

For all of it.

22.

The text from Madeline, suggesting they go out after work, came as a bit of a surprise. Stark had been ready to wrap things up for the night. His head was mashed with the details of the fraud case and he'd spent a thoroughly uninspiring hour in the company of the Procurator Fiscal, Martin McInally. A nice enough guy, but a bit of a pompous old fart, who insisted on talking him through the prosecution's case, coaching him on how to deal with the defence lawyer's likely lines of attack. It wouldn't have been a hard decision to agree to the offer anyway but such a mind-numbing preamble made it all the more welcome.

They met in a newly opened bar-cum-restaurant in Alloa. It was part of a chain and, as such, the interior was a cut and paste from a generic, company blueprint. It was fine, though – convenient for Madeline being just up the street from the bank and, to his great relief, pretty quiet as well.

She greeted him with a hug and a continental-style double peck on the cheek. He would have given anything for a full-on snog instead. They ordered a couple of drinks and took a table at the window, watching the world go by on what was a pleasant evening. Pinks and oranges highlighted the underside of high cloud as the sun began to set.

"How have you been, then?" asked Madeline, tucking her hair behind her ear in that way he found so enchanting.

"Aye, alright. Busy, mind you, but good. You?"

"Yeah, good. I was given an audit by some Head Office bods today. Always a bit stressful but we got a clean bill of health, so all's well."

"That's grand."

"Uh huh, so after they'd packed up and gone, I thought, why not give that rather casual polis I know a ring – see if he can be bothered to come out for a wee drink to celebrate?" She smirked and raised her glass.

He laughed and clinked glasses with her. "Cheers!"

"Are you hungry?" she asked.

"I could eat a scabby horse."

"Right, well, horse is a possibility, I suppose, but I'm not sure how scabby it'll be."

"Magic, let's find out shall we?"

They grabbed some menus and when they'd decided what they wanted, Stark went up to the bar to order.

***

Barr took the call as he stepped out of the car in front of the farmhouse.

"Detective Barr?"

"Aye."

"This is Janet Gibson from the Sports Centre."

"Oh, right, hello again. What can I do for you, Janet?"

There was a pause before she continued and Barr thought for a moment they might have been cut off. "After you'd gone, I got thinking about that person who set off the fire alarm. It was annoying me and I thought I'd look through the footage from this morning to see them leaving. That way, if they dared to show their face in here again, I could mark their card and let them know how unacceptable it was for them not to tell someone what they'd done. Let them know how much of an inconvenience they'd caused, the cost, the potential danger. All that sort of stuff. You know?"

"Uh huh, so did you work out who they were, then?" asked Barr.

"Well, it turns out the person who set the alarm off was a middle-aged, blonde woman. She went out into the car park and got into the driver's side of that silver Golf the lad you were looking for left in."

Barr felt his head swim. "What? Really?"

"Yes, I'm definite it was the same car because I watched the clip with the boy in it again to make sure. It was definitely the same car. I wasn't sure if it meant anything, or if it would help you in any way, but I thought I better tell you just in case."

"No, no, you were right to let me know, Janet. Thanks. You've been very helpful. Cheerio the now."

"Ok, that's good, glad to help out. I hope you manage to find the lad. Bye for now, Detective."

Barr looked around. It was a beautiful setting with the hills looming up behind the farm and the small town of Alva laid out below it. The farmhouse was of stone construction; set over two floors, with large, sash windows, a rustic front door and a slate roof. The silver Golf was parked on the driveway out front, which was a good sign. The sun had slipped below the horizon and darkness was on its way. He could see a light on somewhere in the back of the upstairs, which was an even better sign that someone was home.

He wasn't sure what this new information might mean. Did this woman, Sara Glass, set off the alarm on purpose, as a ruse to lure Colin Cook out to her car? If so, why? What was he to her? It was also still nagging at him that she could have been a witness to Paul Jacobs' accident but did nothing to help him or report it. Why would she have done that? What connection did she have to these two lads?

On the other hand, maybe her bumping into the alarm panel really was just an accident, with her meeting and then driving off with the Cook boy being completely spontaneous and unrelated?

Barr felt unsure of how to tackle the approach to the house. Was the lad in there with her now? Was he about to emerge all hot and bothered from an all-day session with his very own Mrs Robinson and just cause embarrassment all round?

It was no good, there was something not right here and he needed to get to the bottom of it. He walked up to the door and rang the bell.

Sara froze, a look of puzzled annoyance crossed her face. She put her finger to her lips and turned off the taps. She tore off a large strip of tape and held it between both thumbs and forefingers.

"Shh, Coco. Let's just ignore them, shall we. I'm not expecting visitors."

The water had stopped just short of lapping up over his mouth and nose. He shifted himself, trying to get a bit more clear of it.

Down at the front door, Ian Barr waited for an answer but none came. He rang the bell again and stepped back from the front door, looking in through the windows, trying to see if anyone responded inside.

Sara put her finger on her lips again when the second ring sounded. "They'll soon get the message and go away, Coco."

Colin was torn. Whoever this was at the door, he didn't want to expose them to this mad, psychotic bitch but, on the other hand, if he didn't cry out and get some help, she was going to kill him. He was in no doubt about that now. He screamed for help and she reacted with fury, sealing his mouth with the tape and pushing his head under the water.

"Bad boy, Coco. Bad boy. Now you're going to feel exactly what it was like for my Davey."

Barr heard the manic shriek from Colin Cook and reacted. He took out his radio and called in for assistance. His instincts had been right – something bad was happening in there and he needed to get in and help whoever that was who just screamed for help. He took a run at the door and shouldered it but it wouldn't budge. He tried again but only succeeded in giving himself a dead arm. He took a brick from the front garden and smashed the nearest window, reached inside and lifted it up.

Colin was struggling as hard as he could but he was losing the fight. She was unnaturally strong and he was already exhausted from all his previous attempts to break free. When the sound of the window smashing downstairs reached them, she released him and disappeared. His relief was short-lived when he realised she'd started the taps running again as she fled. The water rose much quicker this time, and he struggled to lift his head up out of the water as it filled the bath.

Barr clambered in through the window and drew his pepper spray. He could hear water running into a bath from upstairs; some splashing too.

"Hello, Mrs Glass, this is the police. Please let me know everything is alright. Hello? Colin? Colin Cook? Are you here, son? Are you ok?"

He made his way into the front hallway and began to climb the stairs, the splashing from the bathroom was louder now and something about the incoherent noises accompanying it unnerved him. Barr quickened his pace. The bathroom door was open in front of him as he reached the top landing. The sight that greeted him rocked him back on his heels. Colin Cook was bound and gagged and being drowned in the bath as it filled up around and over him. Barr rushed forward to free the boy and felt a dull thud across the back of his head. Everything spun and whirled around him, his legs folded like they'd been transplanted from a new-born foal and he fell face-first onto the bathroom floor.

23.

Stark was just about to order when his phone rang. He took it out and cursed it before accepting the call.

"Hello, sir. This is PC McKay. Sorry to bother you but we've had an urgent call for assistance from DC Barr an' I thought you'd want to know."

"Shit. Really? Have you got any more details, McKay?" asked Stark, stepping out into the street to avoid any eavesdroppers.

"He was at a farmhouse in Alva, sir. Ochil Farm. Said there was a possible kidnapping and assault in progress and required urgent assistance, eh. We've sent a couple of uniform over but I've not heard what's happened since that."

"Right, I'm on my way, McKay. If you hear anything else, let me know. I'll have my radio when I get back to my car."

"Ok, sir, will do."

Stark cancelled the call and went back into the bar.

"Madeline, I'm really sorry, I need to go. There's an emergency at work. Ian Barr might be in a bit of bother an' I need to go an' make sure he's ok."

She looked up at him with concern but also resignation. "Oh, god, that's not good. I hope he's alright?"

"I'm sure he will be, but I have to go. Sorry." He leaned over the table and kissed her on the lips, lingering for a second before breaking it off. They looked at each other for an agonising moment before she broke the spell.

"Go! I'll be fine. Phone or text when you can."

"Thanks. Sorry."

Stark ran from to his car and drove like a maniac towards Alva.

As he turned into the lane that led up to the farmhouse, he could see the blue lights of an ambulance and a squad car swirling through the night. He felt his gut tighten, braced himself for whatever he was about to encounter.

He pulled up and got out of the car. An ashen-faced, female PC approached him and he took out his warrant card.

"DI Stark, what's going on? What's happened to DC Barr? Is he ok"

"He's in the ambulance, sir."

"Fuck! Is he alright?"

"I'm not sure, sir. He took a bad knock to his head. I tried to stop the bleeding but he was unconscious when I got to him. I think the paramedics are getting ready to take him to the hospital."

Stark went over to the ambulance and looked in. The paramedics were securing Barr. He was in a neck brace and as far as Stark could tell, still unconscious. One of the paramedics turned to look at him.

"DI Stark. I'm his boss. Is he going to be ok?"

"We're not sure. He's taken a severe blow to the head. Skull could well be fractured, we need to get him to hospital and get him scanned asap, make sure there's no clots or haemorrhages."

Stark felt queasy.

"Who did it? Do you know?" Stark asked.

"No, but it wasn't the poor fucker in the bath, that's for sure. Some very nasty shit went down in that house tonight an' I think you better get on wi' finding the sick bastard that did it before they kill someone else," said the driver as he climbed out and closed the doors on Barr and his colleague who'd be looking after him on the way to hospital.

"Killed? What are you talking about? Who's been killed?"

"No idea who he is, mate, but I do know he's dead. He'd been tied up in the bath upstairs. We tried to resuscitate him, but without luck."

"In the bath?" asked Stark, frowning.

" Aye, an' drowned in it by the looks of things," shouted the driver as he got into the cab and drove away.

"Holy, fucking, shit!" muttered Stark as he strode towards the house.

The stairs were sodden and squelched underfoot as he climbed them. The other PC who'd been despatched to help Barr walked with him.

"It's a young man, sir. He's naked, got no identification on him. He was tied to the bath an' then drowned in it, eh. I've never seen anything like it, sir. It's sick. When I got here, the front door was wide open an' water was running down the stairs an' into the garden. I ran up there an' found DC Barr lying on the floor, an' this laddie in the bath, eh. I turned off the taps an' pulled out the plug. I tried to free the boy from the ropes but they were tied so tight an' I couldn't …" He stopped talking as they reached the bathroom doorway, a shudder of emotion going through him. The PC was only a kid. Probably just out of Tulliallan. This would have been a tough gig for a seasoned pro, never mind a rookie like him.

"It's ok, son. I'm sure you did your best. I presume he was beyond saving by the time the water drained away?"

"Yes, sir. I managed to cut the ropes wi' a knife from the kitchen an' I tried to revive him, but he was gone. I didn't know what to do, so I left him there on the floor. The paramedics had a go at reviving him but they agreed he was past saving." The lad cleared his throat. "While I was doing all that wi' him, sir, Jenny, err, PC McShane, tried to help DC Barr; made sure his airway was clear, used a towel to try an' staunch the bleeding, an' waited for the paramedics to get here."

Stark followed the crimson stains across the floor and up to the oversized bath. Colin Cook was already going blue; stretched out on the floor, a hand towel placed over him to maintain his modesty. The scene was a total fuck up forensically. At least four people had stomped all over it since Sara Glass made her escape and the body had been moved and handled. Vital evidence could have been compromised but there was nothing else the cops and medics could have done. It was an emergency. There was no time to consider such things when lives were at stake.

He put out an APB for Sara Glass and her silver Golf and made his way back downstairs. The house was sparsely furnished, lacking in any personal touches such as art or photographs. The kitchen was clean and tidy and the food in the cupboards consisted of a few basic supplies. The fridge had a pint of milk and some butter in it. The freezer was empty.

Stark went back out into the fresh air and tried to get a handle on what had happened. Then he remembered Ian Barr's wife. Shit. He had to let her know.

"Kirsty?"

"Aye, is that you, Adam?"

"Aye. Look, Kirsty, I don't want you to panic but it's about Ian. He's been hurt an' they've taken him to Larbert."

"Oh, dear Christ. Is he ok, Adam?"

"I'm sure he's going to be fine but he took a knock to his head. They're taking him in to do some tests an' check him over."

"I need to get over there but I've no' got a car. Ian took it to work wi' him."

Stark could hear her beginning to panic and, in her advanced state of pregnancy, he needed to help minimise her stress levels.

"It's alright, Kirsty, you can't drive the now anyway. I'm sending a PC over to you. She'll take you to the hospital. She should be with you in about fifteen minutes. That should give you enough time to get organised, ok?"

"Aye, thanks, Adam. Are you no' going to be there?"

"No, I need to catch the person responsible. I'll be there as soon as I can, though. He's going to be alright,

Kirsty. He's as tough as they come." He said this as much for his own sake as hers.

"Oh god, I hope so, Adam, eh. I don't know what I'm going to do if he's not."

"Stay strong, Kirsty. It's going to be ok. I've got to get on. Go an' get ready. PC McShane will be with you before you know it."

"Thanks, Adam. Please catch this bastard, eh."

"Oh, I intend to Kirsty, don't worry about that. Bye."

He cut off the call and got in his car. If he thought the call to Kirsty was hard, it would be nothing compared to the one he was about to make to Duncan Cook.

24.

Duncan Cook's devastation manifested itself in the manner Stark thought it would. It was difficult to relay any information to him due to the shouting and demands for action, as well as threats of litigation relating to Stark's and the rest of the force's incompetence. Stark let him vent. It was overwhelming grief expressed via an already naturally overwrought personality. Once the initial wave crashed against the shore, Cook would become more reasonable. At least, that's what Stark hoped would happen.

Once the tirade of ill-will from Duncan Cook had been faced, Stark texted Madeline, apologising for his sudden exit and updating her on the state of play with Ian Barr. Once he'd done that, he began to drive back toward the station, using his hands-free system to call DCI McLaren and update him on what was going on. The boss, like so many others would, found it hard to comprehend. Not that long ago, he'd been indulging in a round of back-slapping and relief at being able to solve the Jacobs and Cook cases. Now, he faced a storm unlike anything he'd faced before. In a provincial town like Alloa, this sort of situation was equivalent to a super-volcano erupting or a devastating flash flood – a once-in-a-hundred-year-event. The Cooks and the press were not likely to be anything other than driven in their pursuit of error or blame. Both brothers had been left childless within the space of a few weeks. That was not something they would allow to fade gently into the background. McLaren would also feel rather foolish in front of his superiors for having convinced them all was well, when it so clearly wasn't. Of course, Stark bore the brunt of his bosses' frustration and discomfiture. It passed through him with as much impact as a radio wave. He'd been in charge of the tee-shirt factory on that one during his time in London and McLaren couldn't even lace Morris Hargreaves' boots when it came to ranting and denigration. To be fair to McLaren, amongst all the abuse, he did enquire after Barr's health and did seem genuinely worried about his junior officer.

Stark was almost back at the station when the radio message came through.

"Alpha Sierra One, this is Sierra Bravo One. Come in. Over."

"Sierra Bravo One, this is Alpha Sierra One. Go Ahead. Over."

"We have reports of a disturbance on the Clackmannanshire Bridge, sir. Assistance requested by traffic division. They think it might be your suspect, Sara Glass. Over."

"Ok, roger that Sierra Bravo One. Am responding. Over and out."

"Message received and understood. Over and out."

Stark switched on his blues and sirens and hammered down his right foot.

The rain started as a spit in the air, barely troubling the wipers but, by the time Stark hit the outskirts of Alloa, it was making more of an effort. He pulled around a dawdling motorist, using terms the person involved might not have found too complimentary if they'd been able to hear them. He barrelled round two roundabouts in quick succession and headed down the dual carriageway towards the bridge. Back to where all this had started.

Ahead of him he could see the traffic guys had set up a road block, their colourful lights cutting into the darkness and precipitation. He came to a halt and opened his window. One of the traffic cops stepped forward and he flashed them his warrant card.

"DI Stark. I'm leading the Sara Glass investigation.

What've you got for me.?"

"We've got an IC1 female threatening to throw herself off, sir. She stopped her car in the middle of the bridge, causing an obstruction, and a member of the public called it in. When we got here, we ran her plates and they matched the APB you issued earlier. We've sealed off the road and one of our girls is trying to talk to her but apart from the threats to jump, she doesn't seem too interested in a conversation or explaining herself."

"Ok, thanks," said Stark, getting out of the car. As the rain hit him, he realised he had no jacket in the car. There was no time to go back for one, so he was just going to have to get wet. Very wet. "Get an ambulance on standby in case she decides to jump. Do you know if we have access to a motor launch or some other boat?"

"I can find out, sir."

"Good, do that as quick as you can. An' what about a life belt or a rope or something like that?"

"Not sure, sir. I'll get someone onto it."

"Right, I'm going to go up an' see if she'll talk to me. I've got things I need to ask her."

The traffic cop watched him walk away towards the bridge and then shouted after him. "Sir, we have a spare waterproof in our car. Do you want it?"

"No, it's ok, thanks. I'm bloody soaked now anyway," said Stark.

As he stepped onto the bridge proper, the wind rushed the rain in to meet him with some force. Ahead he could see the female PC standing on the pathway and the figure of Sara Glass standing on the wrong side of the railing, holding onto the top. Her dark hair was already plastered to her head and she looked to be mumbling to herself. The Golf was parked in the road alongside them.

When he reached the young PC, he told her to retreat so he could deal with things. Her relief was so great he thought she might have hugged him. He moved forward with caution, trying not to spook the woman it turned out had most likely murdered Paul Jacobs, Debbie Cook and Colin Cook, as well as leaving his friend in a bad way.

"Sara?" he said, in a flat, neutral tone.

She turned to look at him and frowned. "Who are you? I told the lassie it was all over, time for me to go. There's nothing will change my mind, pal. Right?"

"Sara, I'm DI Adam Stark. I want to try an' help you. Come back over the rail an' we can talk, eh?"

She shook her head and laughed. "Oh, come on. Talk about obvious. Look, I just told the lassie, it's over, it's time for me to be with Davey. Nothing you say will make any difference to that."

"Davey? Who's Davey, Sara?" He edged a little closer and she reacted.

"Stay where you are! I'm going to jump. I'm going to be wi' Davey. He needs me."

"Who's Davey, Sara?"

"Davey's my boy, my beautiful boy; the one they took from me. But I've made them pay an' now it's time for us to be together again."

"You said *they* took him, Sara. Do you mean Paul Jacobs an' the two Cook kids?"

Her eyes flashed with anger and she took one hand off the rail to jab a finger towards him. "Aye, that's right. Those bastards made his life a misery an' he couldn't take any more, so he … he … but I knew. I knew they did it. *They* made him feel that bad. *They* made him do it. And so I showed *them*. I let *them* know how it felt. How *they* made him feel."

Stark was soaked through to his skin. His clothes clung to him like shrink wrap, and the chilling nip of the wind began to make him shiver. He wished he'd taken up that offer of a waterproof.

"Sara, I'm really sorry about Davey but you killing yourself isn't going to bring him back, is it? Why don't you just climb back over the rail an' we can get you some help?"

"Sorry? Why would you be sorry? You didn't even know who he was. I don't need help, an' I'm no' some daft, wee bairn, DI Stark. I know he's no' coming back. I need to be wi' Davey, an' I'm going where he's already gone. Neither of us is coming back."

"An' what about my colleague, DC Barr? What did he have to do wi' it? You know he's in a critical condition in hospital?" Stark had no idea how Barr was doing but hoped he was wrong and this was only for effect.

Sara Glass looked down at her feet. "I'm sorry about that. I had no choice, eh. He'd have stopped me showing Coco what it was like for Davey. He'd have stopped me finishing things off. I never meant to hurt him badly."

"Aye, well, that's all very well, Sara, but Ian's got a wife an' a couple of bairns. What are they going to do if he dies?"

"Dies? He's no' that bad is he?"

"He's in intensive care. Touch an' go they said." Again, Stark felt a pang of guilt and dread. He wasn't sure he should be tempting fate like that – just so he could convince this woman to climb back over to his side of the barrier and allow him to arrest her.

"Tell his wife I'm sorry," she said and dived off the side of the bridge.

"No!" shouted Stark and charged over to the railing. He couldn't see anything in the dark water below. As the wind tried to steal the last of the warmth from his body, without thinking, he climbed over the railing and jumped in after her.

If he thought the wind was a heat thief, it had nothing on the water. The cold slammed into him like a champion heavyweight's right hand. The black, swirling murk surrounded him and he struggled to find his bearings. Why had he been so impetuous, so stupid? He wasn't even that good a swimmer. He thrashed his arms and legs and tried to find the surface but, in the confusion, he couldn't even work out which way was up or down or sideways. The current was strong and each time he thought he was about to break free from it, it dragged him back again, spinning him over and over. His lungs cried out for the solace of oxygen and he began to get worried. It was so cold.

Stark thrashed again but still didn't find any air. His limbs were heavy, aching. His chest began to heave and his stomach rippled like a belly-dancer's. He couldn't hold on any longer but when he inhaled, real panic overtook him. Water inundated the one area of his body where it was least welcome. He thrashed again but nothing seemed to happen. And again. But, though he tried to stop it, the water kept on going where it wasn't meant to go. His mind became dulled, his limbs stilled and the panic dimmed to a flicker then evaporated. Blackness consumed him and he felt the cold no more.

25.

Stark sat at the bedside, hypnotised by the drip falling from the plastic bag into the tube that carried life-preserving fluids into Ian Barr's bloodstream. He could sense one of those headaches lurking in the background. The ones that had plagued him since waking from his ill-advised swan-dive into the River Forth. The doctors told him he was lucky to have survived the anoxia, and even more so to have come through it without any serious brain damage. The same could not be said for Ian Barr. His prognosis was far from encouraging.

This was the first time Stark had found the strength to get out of his own sick bed to go and visit his stricken colleague. He struggled to come to terms with what the doctor told him. Ian Barr was probably brain dead. The baseball bat caused a massive bleed into his brain and, despite heroic efforts on the part of the surgical team, they feared the damage was too great for him to ever recover from. The swelling was yet to fully subside and, until it did, there was still a glimmer, a chink of hope for Kirsty to hold onto. For now, machinery and electronics controlled his heart and lungs and the drip kept him hydrated and nourished. Stark didn't want to contemplate what this might lead to – the options that would be laid in front of Ian's family if that hope turned out to be misplaced.

"I'll see you in a bit, my friend," he said and got up.

Stark shuffled back to his own bed, stepped out of his slippers and sat on top of the blankets. It was very warm in the ward and he didn't need to sleep. He wasn't one of those folk with a fear of hospitals or a hatred of the smells and atmosphere. He accepted it for what it was. Stark knew he needed to be there so good people could help

187

him to recover. He hoped they'd be able to help Ian Barr. He picked up a music magazine Madeline had left him, flicking through it again, not really reading anything, just trying to distract himself from dark thoughts.

DCI McLaren appeared at his bedside like a Ninja extra from Miami Vice. "Alright Adam, how're you doing?"

Stark almost jumped out of the bed in fright. "Jesus, sir, where the hell did you come from?"

McLaren laughed and dropped the bag of grapes he was carrying onto the bed. "Alloa, where d'you think?"

"Aye, right. Very good," said Stark, ignoring the grapes, which were no use to anybody unless in their fermented, liquid form, as far as he was concerned.

"Good to see you up an' about again, Adam. You gave us all a bloody fright wi' that Greg Louganis impersonation. I mean, what the hell were you thinking about, man?"

Stark shrugged. "I wasn't thinking, sir. It was pure instinct. It happened too quick for me to think anything through. If I had, I wouldn't have done it. Trust me."

"Aye, well, you were lucky – especially compared to that poor bastard Barr," said McLaren, pulling over a chair and sitting down by Stark's bedside. "One bairn still in a pram, an' another on the way any minute, eh. That poor lassie. It's a bloody sin, so it is."

"Aye, it's no' too good, sir," was all Stark could muster in reply.

"Anyway, I came to fill you in on what's been happening while you've been sitting about in here, you lazy bastard." The attempt at humour was welcome and eased the tension between them. It almost felt like a normal conversation between friends.

"First off, you're probably wondering what happened to that crazy bitch who attacked Barr?"

Stark nodded.

"Well, although our guys in the boat managed to fish you out of the water, she wasn't so lucky. She washed up the next day – almost in the exact spot that poor Cook lassie was found."

"Right. An' do we know any more about her, sir? She told me those three kids she killed had been responsible for killing her son, Davey. Was that true?"

"Well, sort of. She was sectioned and hospitalised about eight or nine years back after her laddie committed suicide, eh. He took some pills an' drowned in the bath. In interviews wi' the doctors, she claimed the Jacobs laddie and the Cooks had effectively killed him; bullied him into killing himself, but they decided she was just looking for someone to blame. The school did an investigation but both the Cooks an' Jacobs denied everything an' their parents put pressure on the school to drop it. There weren't the same attitudes to bullying then as there are now."

"So they maybe did bully him?" said Stark.

"Probably. Must have been pretty bad, though, to cause the wee man to top himself."

"And to cause her to do what she did."

"Indeed," agreed McLaren. "She seems to have hidden the homicidal thoughts well enough to be released an' then appears to have spent some considerable time planning what to do wi' the three kids she blamed for her boy's death. The farmhouse was rented but she had this humongous bath installed about three months ago without the landlord's permission. She must have been following them about, waiting for the right moment to strike."

"Do we know what she had to do wi' Paul an' Debbie's deaths, yet?"

"Archie Brown has come up wi' a hypothesis that she stopped Paul Jacobs from getting clear of the water in the ditch. Maybe even actively drowned him. The lassie? Who knows? She might have played the guilt card on her, persuaded her to jump of her own accord or she might have forced her to jump. We'll never be one hundred per cent sure on that. We do know she drowned the Cook laddie in that bath an' then lamped Barr wi' a baseball bat when he tried to stop her."

Stark took a sip of fruit juice from the glass at his bedside and looked up at the ceiling, letting out a huge sigh.

"Anyway, I've met wi' the Cooks an' talked it through. They're a bit less angry wi' us, an' a bit less inclined to seek legal recompense now, what wi' the impending besmirching of their dead kids' good names, what happened to Barr when he was trying to save the boy, an' what happened to you when you were trying to arrest Glass."

"An' what about Sam Jacobs? Have you talked to him?"

"Aye, now, he was a bit more of a problem. Very sharp, very angry. He was particularly upset about how his boy got tarred as a murderer. I think once he saw how Paul was going to be portrayed as a bully, who caused the death of a young boy anyway, it didn't really matter. His life has been wrecked, whatever the truth about Paul. I expect he couldn't see what difference it would make haggling over the finer details."

Stark took another sip of juice. "Thanks for letting me know, sir. It's a bloody tragic mess all round."

"It sure is, Adam. Right, I'm for the off. The HR department will no doubt be in touch about one of them back to work plans, eh. Cheerio the now."

"Aye, cheers, sir. I'll see you back at the ranch before you know it."

McLaren waved over his shoulder as he walked away.

26.

Stark looked down at the little bundle in Kirsty Barr's arms and smiled. "He's going to be smitten when he finally meets her."

Kirsty looked up at him and smiled back. "I can't wait to take her to see him, Adam."

She looked exhausted but, to be fair, ten hours of labour were a good excuse for not looking at your most chipper when visitors came calling.

"When will you get to take her down to him?"

"Doctor said sometime this week. Have to be careful not to overwhelm him, eh. It's going to be a long road back an' we're going to need a huge amount of patience." A tear leaked from the corner of her eye and she wiped it away with a sniff.

Stark squeezed her hand. "Anything you need, Kirsty, you just ask. Right?"

She looked up at him and nodded. No words would come.

"Anyway, I better be getting away, now. You take care, an' give Ian my best when you see him. Let me know when the rest of us are allowed to visit. Ok?" She nodded again as he leant down and kissed the baby on the head. "See you later little lady."

Stark walked down the corridor, out the door, into the car park and sat down in the passenger seat of Madeline's very nice company BMW. She reached over and hugged him, kissing his neck. "How are they?"

"Yeah, pretty good, considering," he said. "It's going to be tough, though. Ian's still in a bad way an' we've no idea how much permanent brain damage he's suffered. The doctors are naturally cautious. They don't like to get your hopes up or leave themselves open to accusations later, you know. But, no matter what happens, I think they're going to be ok."

"That's good, babes. Do you want to go home now?"

"Aye, let's go an' get something to eat. Can we just run past my Ma's place first? I've got a couple of things to pick up."

"No bother."

Stark stood at the gate of his mother's house and looked at the for sale sign. One of the neighbours waved and he returned the gesture. He knew this was the right time to do this. He knew it's what she'd want and expect of him but he couldn't help the trace of melancholy it brought on. It was daft, really. This wasn't where he grew up and his father had never lived there before his death. And yet, somehow, letting it go affected him more than he thought it might when he and Madeline agreed to sell their respective properties and buy somewhere together.

He turned the key in the lock and walked through the hall to the kitchen. He rummaged around in one of the drawers and retrieved the set of photos he'd been thinking about that day. Snaps of the four of them in happier times. If he was moving out, they were coming with him. The furniture, the pictures, the bedding and soft furnishings were staying there to help buyers get a sense of what the place could look like. The chances were the target market was another retired woman or couple. When it did sell, he'd give all those fripperies away to charity or take it down to the dump. Another pang of loss tugged at him but it would pass. In truth, he would be happy to take this furniture to their new home but he knew Madeline shouldn't have to indulge his nostalgia; his irrational attachment to things that were of no real importance. He had to concentrate on the here and now, not wallow in the past and the if onlys.

Closing the door, he walked back up the path and got

back into the car.

"Let's go," he said. "That dinner isn't going to eat itself, you know."

Madeline smiled that magical smile and Stark knew he had to do better this time. This time, he had to hold onto her, to make her the priority. The recovery time in the hospital and his near-death experience had hardened his resolve to make positive change in his life. He might have loved being a copper but he was pretty sure he loved her more.

He just had to prove it.

THANK YOU!

Thank you for buying this book - I really hope you enjoyed it. If you did, it would be great if you could leave a review on Amazon, Goodreads or your favourite social media site.

You can visit my website at *petercarroll.ravencrestbooks.com*, and while you are there, I'd be delighted if you also subscribed to my blog. That way, I can keep you up to date with future books and other writing adventures.

Look out for my other novels *In Many Ways, Pandora's Pitbull, Drivers, Stark Contrasts* and *Stark Choices* which are all available on Amazon Kindle and in paperback.

All the best
Peter

ALSO BY PETER CARROLL

In Many Ways   getBook.at/IMW

Pandora's Pitbull   getBook.at/pandora

Drivers   getBook.at/drivers

Detective Inspector Adam Stark novels
Stark Contrasts   getBook.at/starkcontrasts

Stark Choices   getBook.at/starkchoices

CONTACT DETAILS

Visit the authors website:
petercarroll.ravencrestbooks.com

twitter.com/petercarroll10

facebook.com/PCNovel1

Cover designed by: Raven Crest Books

Cover photography by © Alan Gray
alangrayimages.com/

Published by: Raven Crest Books
ravencrestbooks.com

Like us on Facebook:
facebook.com/ravencrestbooksclub

About The Author

Peter is a Scottish person who's nearer fifty than forty now and has no idea how that happened! He's been married for a long time and has one daughter. When finances and time permit, he travels the world in search of birds and other wildlife and is a committed conservationist. As a self-taught bassist, saying he's a musician may be stretching it, but he has a go now and again.

Literary influences include Christopher Brookmyre, Stephen King and Irvine Welsh, so expect bad language, violence, black humour and significantly fewer adverbs than most...oh...